THE
X-MAS
FILES

THE X-MAS FILES

RICHARD ANTALL

atmosphere press

© 2021 Richard Antall

Published by Atmosphere Press

Cover design by Ronaldo Alves

No part of this book may be reproduced without permission from the author except in brief quotations and in reviews. This is a work of fiction, and any resemblance to real places, persons, or events is entirely coincidental.

atmospherepress.com

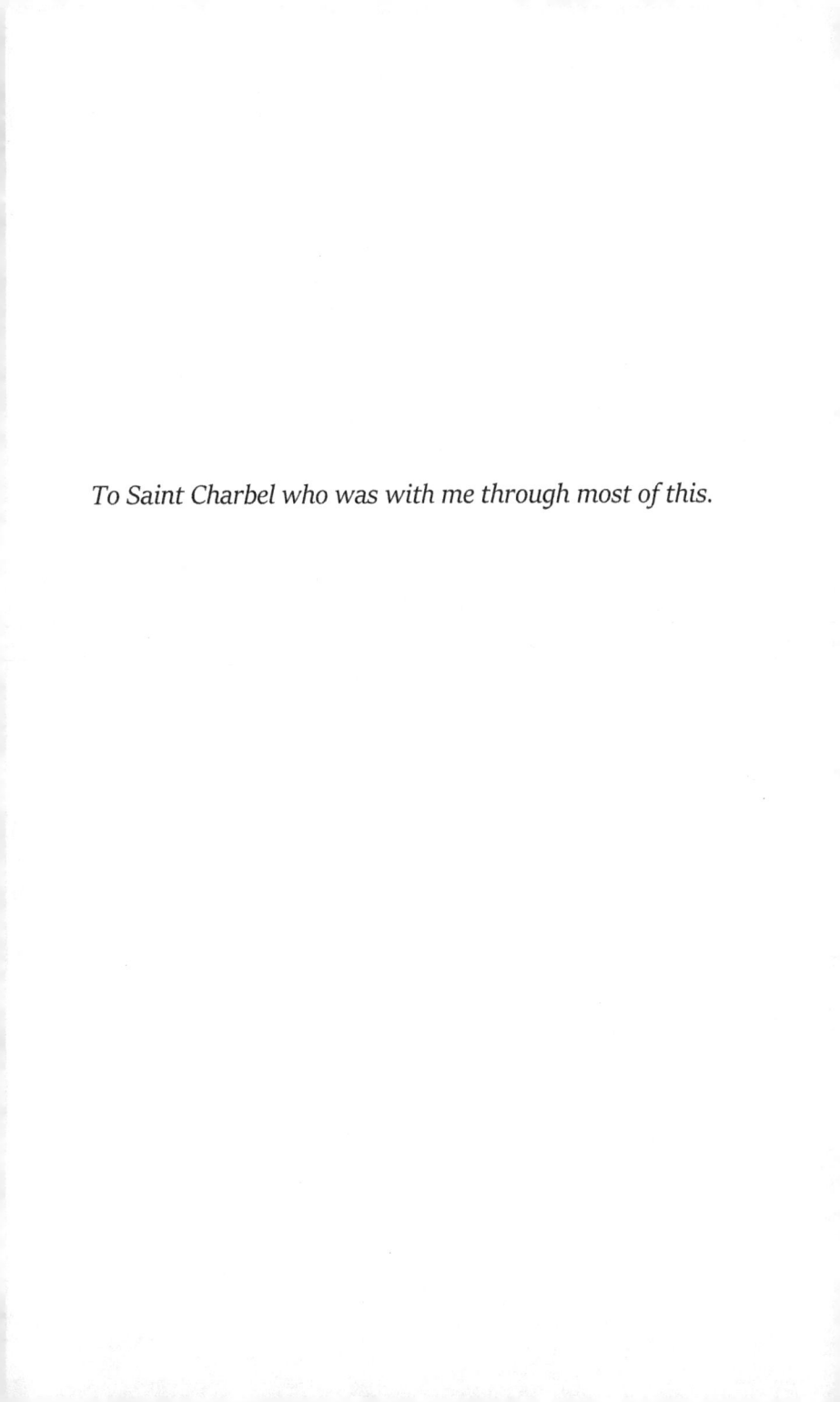

To Saint Charbel who was with me through most of this.

*"An apology for the Devil: it must be remembered that
God has written all the books."*
Samuel Butler II Note-Books

PREFACE

I cannot tell you in detail how I came across these files. The person who is responsible for smuggling them out is now safe from any harm, so it is not as though I were obliged to take measures to protect him. In fact, he is in a quite secure place, a witness protection program called Purgatory. At least I think he is there, on the basis of his last confession, which I heard punctuated by a cough I would call infernal even under other circumstances. He seemed to me truly repentant, and he had much to be repentant about. Unfortunately, he died before I could give him the apostolic blessing and plenary indulgence.

He didn't have much time to tell me the mechanics of how he was able to come upon these files and actually translate them from the ancient tongue of the angels. Although he tried to explain some of the details, he could see that he was speaking a language just as difficult as the angelical one for me. He told me that to say the ancient language of the angels was a metaphor did not imply that angels have a language like ours—which of course they don't. It was something like two computers talking to each other, but with a perfect harmony and congruence between ideas and reality. How that perfection is possible is beyond our human comprehension, of course. I suppose it would be something like living outside of Plato's Cave, as far as communications go.

At any rate, the party in question was more interested in receiving pardon for his sins and renewing sanctifying grace than in giving me a tutorial about the infernal edge of the Internet. I can say no more about the technical aspects of this revelation, except that I sense that the personage we call the Prince of This World was very unhappy in that hour.

The young man (relatively, which means in my dialect that he was not yet forty) had got involved in some very strange and ugly things. He was a computer specialist, one of those "hackers," but a genius even among them. That is why he had been hired at what I consider a princely salary by a prominent firm of those that come to Ireland for tax relief purposes. Somehow he had managed to hit upon some of the internal communication systems that "His Satanic Majesty" (as he is called in infernal officialese) has sewn into the seams of the Internet. I suppose that this was initially through some type of pornographic search engine. The benighted man was a genius, but very sick emotionally. He told me that he had learned German, Dutch, and Japanese just in order to download more pornographic pictures and videos of the most unspeakable human and/or animal acts. (Later he learned Chinese, but I think that was with the devil's help.)

Once he was online with the devil, he was assigned his own Mephistopheles. This M, as he signed some correspondence, arranged a contract by which the man signed over the rights to his soul in a Faustian bargain that gave him a power in the communication superhighway that beggars the imagination, to use a fine old phrase. Not only did he have access to others' computers and thus their private lives, but also could do everything he desired, from robbing cyber fortunes to delaying planes to starting small wars. He did not want fame but easily could have been the most famous man in the world. He preferred a type of cyber imperium and fancied himself an invincible Bin Laden, holed up in an invisible Pakistan and beyond the reach of nations and their corporate sponsors. All of this somehow disappeared, and I wonder if there is a fortune on the books in a Swiss bank owned by someone no one will ever hear about who just disappeared.

So cyber Croesus was on top of the world. Then his mother died. She had been an old-time-religion Catholic lady whose prayers from beyond the grave must have made possible the conversion of her rebel son. It was my pastoral duty to give Christian burial to the good woman. Mr. X, as I prefer to call the Informant of these things, came to me to ask whether he could take her rosary from the casket before we closed it. He had the impression that it was a great favor that I suggested substituting a rosary I carried in my pocket and put it in the hands of the dead woman. Thus he kept her rosary as a keepsake that was the key to his liberation from the diabolical chains he had accepted. At the time, I just thought him odd. Grief brings out the strangeness in us sometimes.

A few days after the funeral, he began calling me. Several times he hung up as soon as I answered. Then he would speak and talk vaguely of "doing something" in memory of his mother. It was obvious he needed a talk. Eventually, I convinced him to come to see me. His collapse in my office resulted in his final hospital stay. Apparently his health had been greatly debilitated by the strenuous sinfulness of his last years and the final crisis resulted in "all the systems shutting down," as he put it.

It was in the hospital, under the plastic crucifix that still hangs in the rooms of an institution that has little to do with Catholicism, that I was able to hear his confession. With what was literally his dying breath, he told me where to find the keys to a condominium on Parnell Street in Dublin where I found in a safe a thumb drive that contained the history that I publish at this time. I know that I will be doubted in this regard. If I were asked my opinion of a story like that I am telling here, I would respond with the most profound caution. However, I feel that not to publish would be the greatest error in my life. The *contretemps* I experienced in getting this book to print are for me a sign that I have done the right thing in offering this information to the public. His Satanic Majesty certainly did not want this little book published. I eschew the histrionic, but in fact cannot refrain from telling you that two literary agents and three editors disappeared or died or took sick mysteriously in the course of this book's path to publication. Only Divine Providence can explain how I was able to offer you what you are reading in this moment.

I was visited by a strange character after my first attempts to find a publisher interested in the papers. He was as smooth as butter left out on a summer's day. Nice suit, no wrinkles at all, which surprised me because he had supposedly driven from Dublin to see me. Did I know a Mr. X? he wondered. "I might," I told him. My memory did not always serve me, I said. A priest runs into a lot of people.

Well, he said, Mr. X used to work with him. Sad case, really. Mental illness, genius and madness close aligned, etc. Obviously, the poor man was not in his right mind. Claimed all sorts of strange things and with a paranoia that was practically otherworldly. While he was saying this, the man had his beady eyes on me like a hawk that has spotted a young chicken. I felt such a disquiet that I looked up at the crucifix in my office suddenly and when I looked back at him, his head was down. That tipped me off.

What could I do for the man? I asked. He wondered, he said, if the man had talked crazy to me. I listen to a lot of people is how I responded. Did X. give me anything? What would he have given me? I asked. Maybe a donation, because X. had a great deal of money. This was the purpose of the visit, trying to sort out whom X. might want to receive some of the cash he left, Paypal accounts or something. I didn't know of such things, I told him. Or maybe X. had talked to me of some papers. The "poor soul" was mad about conspiracies, talked all sorts of nonsense about the Internet, even things about the devil. X. was some kind of an author, writing obsessively, stuff that was absurd, like science fiction. Did I ever hear of Kafka? the gray-suited man asked me.

I had heard of him, I said.

If Kafka were a madman, incoherent, totally divorced from reality, he would have produced some of what X. wrote, pure "madness," said my visitor. I am not sure why the fellow wanted to throw Kafka into the mix, but it makes me wonder about that writer's salvation.

There was something about this "man who knew X." that unnerved me. I felt a chill in the air and his insinuations were frightening to me. If I ever received from X. any writings, I should hand them over, he said. It might help his family. As far as I knew, there had only been his mother, but I said nothing—fish die because of their mouths is a saying in the Romance languages. He went on. The police were interested also. In the midst of his madness, X. had committed larceny against his company and against individuals. Even some government information was compromised, he said, nodding gravely at me. Was I quite sure X. never gave me anything to look at?

It was stretching the truth a bit, but I said that I never received anything written from X. The man seemed surprised. "Nothing? No documents?"

"Not a single sheet of paper," I replied.

He looked at me and, while not satisfied with my answer, did not seem to want to alienate me. I put my hand into my pocket and touched my rosary beads. The man started as though an electric shock had gone through him.

"Some of what X. stole was intellectual property," he said.

"I have no idea of what you are talking about," I said.

Very subtly, I brought my hand up to my chest and felt my medals through my shirt. One of them is a very large one of St. Benedict. Again, the man almost jumped from the chair. I concluded that I was entertaining a representative from hell.

"You know he was crazy, I am sure," the man said. "Stark raving, paranoid. No doubt he told you many absurd things."

His gaze no longer met my eyes.

"Because of the seal of confession, I really can't talk

about what we spoke of," I said.

This was met with a puzzled look. There was silence for a long minute.

"Well, I appreciate your visit, Mr...." I said.

"Dahak," he said, as he stood because I was on my feet.

"I really must be over to the church," I said. "My holy hour."

He winced and then sighed.

"If we could recover any of this intellectual property I am speaking about, we would be able to make a substantive donation to your parish," he said.

"Indeed, then I wish he had given me something," I said.

"It could be on a thumbnail drive," he said.

"You're speaking Greek to me," I said.

I wanted to say, Away Satan, because I had recognized the name he gave from the *Brewer's Dictionary of Phrase and Fable* which is practically my constant companion. *Dahak* was the Persian devil slated to reign one thousand years before *Ormuzd* would introduce a kingdom of peace. No doubt the poor devil took me for an ignorant priest who would not recognize the name. I escorted him out to his car with a bottle of holy water in my hand. He looked at it warily, but I did not use it. He was gone. I ran into the house to spray the chair he had sat in with holy water.

The pages that follow are taken from some kind of infernal journalism, an essay about the mistakes made by the various devils assigned to Palestine at the time of the Incarnation. The author apparently had access to what I would call the Undernet's (or should it be the Evilnet's?) archives of hell that include reports about the work of all the bad angels since Adam and Eve. It is a kind of composite work, and there seem to be various hands on the different chapters. The narrative strains for what I guess could be called "infernal orthodoxy," but you can tell that there are stories behind this story. The hellish quality of the history is seen in how the historians try to convince themselves that they can still win. It reminds me a bit of the kind of rhetoric Hitler was spouting even as the enemy armies were closing in on Berlin. That is, except, in this case, it would be the work of underlings who seem to be both terrified of HSM (as Satan is known in these pages) and of the fact that the whole idea of their victory is impossible. It is an endgame situation and they know they are losing. What they hope for is as many damages to third parties (that is: you and me) as possible. It is the supernatural equivalent of the scorched earth tactics of the Nazis as they retreated from Russia.

From the notes left by the Informant, I deduce that the "report" as it called itself both was and was not an official government white paper sort of thing. There is always the devil in details. I am old enough to remember the Pentagon Papers and have some awareness of the WikiLeaks business. So this collection of documents—I call them chapters, like my penitent did—represents a diabolical dossier. These chapters *seem* to be an attempt to write an official history, a kind of whitewashing of what must be a most painful memory for the diabolic regime. However, "ambiguity, thy name is hell." The caprice of the sovereign power in Inferno made any "official" history provisional. Revisionism is the devil's forte.

These papers are a kind of Inferni-leaks, a demonic spin on "why we lost the war (so far)" and neither you nor I should have been able to read them. There is evidence that the papers were a work in progress, revised periodically by Hell's Intelligence Community. Mister X smiled when he said that the documents had a kind of samizdat *succès de scandale* in the nether regions. Some of the chapters even seem to be in the bastard genre called "podcast." From what I understood amid the staccato coughing of X., His Satanic Majesty did not give it authorization but permitted its circulation, despite its possibly negative aspects in terms of the Eternal War between Heaven and Hell, in order, apparently, to make superior officers afraid of future errors. Even among the damned there is such a thing as reputation, and it stings to be a damned fool even more than just being damned.

So here are some of the secrets of hell itself. My nephew, who is a clever lad but unfortunately seems to be lacking in real grounding in the faith, suggested that the chapters I told him were a kind of "alternative history." I answered him, "Alternative lies, you mean." The relentless infernal propaganda reminds me of some of the Yank media outlets these days, but I am no expert because I have cancelled cable television and don't bother to read the papers besides the sports pages.

Occasionally, I have made some notes to the text. Obviously, something written for angels has a tendency to assume a greater grasp of history and culture than most of us would even pretend to have, although there are some exceptions to this pretension among certain faculties of theology in some famous universities. The ordinary IQ of a devil is thousands of points higher than our own. The prose exhibited is a translation, but the poor man's Faust whom it was my duty to reconcile to God said he had migraines working on the equivalences and what he called the "analogous concepts." I myself cannot say that I understand what the Informant called the "extraordinary demonic irony" of the thing. Thanks be to God, my contact with demons has not been of the sort to permit me to appreciate the nuances of devilish rhetoric. Nevertheless, I imagine that some of the readers of the book will be among those who are able to savor such things.

I close with the presumption to ask you to pray for our Informant. It was the reason he wanted this book published. "They will pray for me," he said in a hoarse whisper that my aural memory declines to stop recalling—I hear it in my dreams. I hope that he is right.

Zbigniew Calvey, Achill Island, Mayo. Eire (this may or may not be my name and whereabouts)

BY WAY OF INTRODUCTION

[This title was the Informant's description of this chapter. It does not appear that he was able to download or whatever you call it the whole book. –ed.]

The spectacular failure of the Palestinian Theater of the War is the subject of this study. I intend to prove that, while the success of the Invasion owed something to the surprise tactics of the Incarnate Enemy (who apparently knows no shame), but also to the egregious errors of strategy by some of our *illustrious* generals. These generals were in charge of "Holding the Line," but didn't because of incompetence complicated by their selfish indulgence, blind ambition, and the traitorous competition that existed between them.

The High Command had never forgotten that the worst was expected to come from Palestine. The territory of the Jews and Samaritans and the regions nearby were positively infested with demons. One third of the Infernal Forces was directly assigned to the Palestinian Theater for at least two millennia. There were so many devils present that it was common for more than one demon to take up lodging in a human being. One benighted soul, of whom it was predicted a role close to the Messiah, was infested with more than one thousand demons. The disaster of that particular operation would merit its own study, but it is not part of the scheme of these notes. Perhaps the most important point is that it was not for lack of troops that our side lost the spectacular battle to the Incarnate Enemy, but because of poor use of the same.

Somehow, it was thought that sheer numbers would prevent the Invasion. What was really necessary, as we all know now thanks to the discourses of His Satanic Majesty, was more strategic placement of the anti-invasion forces. Obviously, it could be argued that the Enemy attacked in the most unspeakable of manners, disguised in a humiliation we thought beyond even His very low standards. However, it was known beforehand that the Invasion would take place. It could have (should have) been stopped while still in its infancy. In this regard I refer the reader to the speeches of His Satanic Majesty. [There followed a long stream of numbers, some sort of archival cross-reference, but nothing helpful to you the reader. – ed.] It is clear that there was irresponsibility among subordinates. If HSM had been obeyed, the war situation would be quite different.

This is not to admit to the Michaelist heresy that pretends to say that our side is inevitably lost. Although it can be documented that HSM has never said that there was infiltration in the Revolution, neither has he ever said the contrary. There could have been and could be within our ranks secret agents of the Other Side. These devils would really be angels committed to serve the Trinitarian Tyranny but in disguise among us. Most likely, these would be found in the order of angels. I say this because it appears to me that the other ranks are too well controlled to admit infiltration: the bottom of the pyramid is the broadest base and the building blocks inspected with less care. Among the angels who joined the Revolution, it is possible that some have been only feigning rebellion. These have conspired to frustrate some of the greatest operations planned by HSM. The "Infiltration Hypothesis" has had its ups and downs, but is still quite a functional one. It explains how many times defeat has been plucked from the mouth of victory, to the chagrin and loyal outrage of those most identified with the Kingdom of Darkness. [Paranoia with a whiff of sulfur. –Informant]

The Michaelists are not simply those who say that there has been Infiltration. Rather, they are the Enemy *Within* who concedes that all our actions are those of an army in retreat; that we can only hope to delay the final victory of the Kingdom of Light, to use the atrocious metaphor that has been applied to the repressive powers in league with the Trinitarian Tyranny. The true Michaelists hiding among us are those who believe we have already lost the war, no matter how many side-battles remain to be won. The desire to "go down fighting" that some of the leaders of the heresy professed in their trials is nothing but a case of pitiful self-excusing. As HSM put it, "The exaggerations of certain parties whose interests have been to discourage the Revolution cannot be forgiven 'because of their making some routine verbal genuflections at the altar of self-oblation.' So they pretend to great loyalty who say we fight a losing battle? They say that this is a kind of existential mystery? Let them meditate upon this mystery in the last Circle, choking, etc." [I would rather not make explicit this rather grotesque message, especially because it is an example of what the Informant called an 'anthropomorphic style.' –ed.]

Nevertheless, it is not within the scope of this study to disprove the basic thesis of the Michaelist Infiltration. This would take much more than this study of the bad leadership in the Palestinian Theater at the time of the Invasion. It would require that the researcher be given access to archives now practically inaccessible. Besides that, anyone who believes in the ability of the Supreme Commander to defeat the sycophant forces around the throne of the TT [An abbreviation for the Trinitarian Tyranny. –Informant] need not worry about the dangers of conspiracies that are bound to fail. If HSM were concerned, he would put a crack team onto the question. If he has not, it is because it is not a real concern. *Faith in our leadership will carry the day! He is the One who truly knows! Dare to follow him who will not serve!* [These are demonic equivalents, apparently, of *"Heil Hitler"* and punctuate the narrative at various places. I do not always include them in the text. –Informant]

The sources that I have consulted for this work are diverse. *The History of the Seraphim Rebellion (HSR)* has several chapters on the Invasion time. The archives of the Cherubim Anti-Tyrannical Liberation Army (ACATLA) also have information that is very useful. The respective histories prepared by the Thrones, Dominations and Powers, although somewhat tendentious, still have some nuggets of information that proved to be essential. The role of the Virtues in the complicated scenario involving the visit of the Persian Magi has made their court-martial of Ursheol controversial. It is apparent that there may be more to that story than once understood. I refer the interested to the latest speech of HSM on the subject of the "Problems with Courts-Martial When They Do Not Reflect the Sovereign Will of the Supreme Leader but Only the Capricious Will of Some Who Would Subvert the Revolution Pretending to Know What They Don't."

Since I am a Principality in rank, my order has proportioned to me all the information in our official archives as well as the time to do this research. I am profoundly grateful to our leader Field Marshal Malignitas for all of his support during this period. He has protected me from threats and several attempts to blackmail me by individual spirits who (I assure all) will suffer the consequences of the same.

Individual angels have helped me with certain elements of the narrative. As the patient reader will soon find out, this investigation is a work of reconstruction. Anything of this scope has to be a work of redaction, and many hands went into its making. It is not true, as some of the envious have said, that I used the work of humans to build my case against the Palestine Occupation Forces. Of course, I did consult the stories collected in the book of the Covenant; it would be quite ignorant not to do so. The humans are not completely devoid of intellect, and we all know that they had help in the writing of *their* materials. Since their works were intended for a human audience, however, there is much that was left out. The presumptuous style characteristic of the stories did not permit their authors to let on how close the Invasion danced to failure in the first few months. *And let us not forget that we still control the world!*

I dedicate this work of investigation to the Supreme

Commander of Our Revolution, His Satanic Majesty the Archdevil Lucifer. Obviously, I write it in the hope that he will be better served by his subordinates in the future and as a lesson to all of the consequences of failure in our duty to serve Him Who Would Not Serve Another. *May he reign forever! Eternal Revolution! We Will Not Cede! The Field Is Won! No Retreat! Arbeit macht frei! Etc.*

Of course, when we are seeking to blame the ridiculous actions of some traitorous demons, we should not forget that the Invasion as such was beaten back. We should not be afraid of all the talk of *You Know Who*'s "Son" coming back. As our Esteemed Leader has said, "There is a Latin expression—I like using the language of the Roman Pretenders—"qui fugiebat rursus proeliabitur." This means that he who fights and runs away can come back and try to fight again. I suppose that is what the Adversary intends. But this is no more than the words of the defeated. This "I shall return" business is not something everyone needs to believe. It is like the myth of the return of the correct strand of the royal family to a benighted land in the north of Europe—a place that has practically been in our hands for centuries. "Wait for me," He says. *Wait for Samuel Beckett,* we say. As a client state of ours experienced it, certain imperial forces made a tragic mistake of a porcine harbor. [Perhaps this refers to the Gadarene demoniac. -Informant] Why should the Enemy come back in glory, when He was defeated the first time? "He ran away the first time, leaving only some weak insurgent forces, etc., etc."

[I have included one of the egregious errors of the Informant's commentary because I think it actually makes the report more convincing. A young man, at least compared to the one who edits this manuscript, he did not recognize the reference to the Bay of Pigs. He was translating from Angel into English, and his literalness tripped him up. He confided to me that he found the speeches of Satan quite turgid and difficult to translate because of their overblown style. It is hard not to notice the unwieldy character of some of the sentences quoted from His Satanic Majesty in the text. –ed.]

At the risk of redundancy, the Invasion was successfully fought back. [Ha! –Informant] That is what we cannot ever forget. Who ended up rejected by the very people He had come to "save"? Who died a humiliating death? However, we should not underestimate the Enemy's resources. The guerrilla forces do not really upset our domination of society in the present age, but they need constant vigilance. Clearly, the century just passed a few decades ago was a triumph. We were able to help Hitler, Lenin, Stalin and Mao, men who will stand the test of evil history. Human life is in more danger than it has ever been before—and that from the very womb. There is not a moment of time from conception to death in which we don't have access to the means of destruction. We have never been so successful in dominating the means of communication between earthlings than we are at present. No place on the planet is immune from the Culture of Death that we have been able to inspire. The world is awash in Sex and Death of the most selfish and cruel kind. How can He dare question our empire?

Hail Satan, etc.!

CHAPTER ONE:
TOUR D' HORIZON

Palestine at the time of the Invasion was a well-cultivated garden of human misbehavior. The Occupation Forces had control of all the important groups in the society. The complicated nature of the Occupation of Palestine requires a kind of panoramic presentation. Each social grouping within the society was under the supervision of a different branch of the Infernal Host. Each of these Coordination Groups was headed by a devil who was automatically a member of the Council on Occupation. The infernal organization was perfect, of course.

[There is evidence of gaps here, indicating some kind of editing. Not all of the document could be recovered. -- Informant]

The Responsible for King Herod was a Cherubim of the name Ursheol. He had an enormous staff and besides Cherubs these included Dominions and Angels. His success with Herod made him one of favorites of the Infernal Court. [There is another great gap here, perhaps related to the story of Luxbel cited below. -Informant]

Ursheol was called "the satrap" by some of his associates and his style was quite imperial, in both the ancient Persian sense and the broader meaning available from examples of human dictatorships that have multinational bases. His celebrated "contests" in which he and his staff competed to see whose client could cause the most havoc were the envy of the Occupation Forces in Palestine. At times, he would invite the Division Commanders to various exhibitions of human degeneracy. The excesses of these events, in which humans would commit any number of mortal sins, were compared to the chariot races of the Coliseum. Each devil would have his particular human and induce him or her to sin. The devil who could inspire his client to the most sins would win.

Of course, Ursheol won every time he competed. Herod was an extreme example of a Slave to Passions. Ursheol was able to convert a dinner party of the court into the preamble of the murder of the king's wife. The cherub's ability to trump the other members of his staff had to do with the enormous power exercised by Herod. "Who can out-Herod Herod?" was the complaint of disgruntled competitors in the contests. At one contest, Ursheol was able to manipulate the great Herod into committing all seven of the Seven Deadly Sins within a period of a few hours. Afterward, the feat was the *beau ideal* of the Occupation Forces.

It was, however, a waste of time and resources. A soul already lost does not have to be lost again. Ursheol argued that the contests sharpened skills, but they also tended to concentrate the attention of agents on a small elite that was already in our control. The problem was that while the officers played with the rich and famous, poor commoners were ignored. This was the principal charge at the trial of Ursheol and Luxbel, which can be verified by reference to the archives of the Supreme Court.

The Pharisees were in the charge of a Seraph named Mardoch. He was assigned by the High Command to Palestine, although his work included supervision of the overseas branches of the movement. Mardoch was sure that the Pharisees were completely under control. Unlike the other devils in the Occupation Forces, he had almost no interest in human sexual behavior. His subjects were beyond that problem, he said. Concupiscence made human beings more subject to our suggestion, he reported to the High Command, but Pride was better for total control over them. "If the Pharisee is proud enough, I can make him resist any grace at all," he said.

In Palestine, he considered himself the second in importance, although his relationship with Ursheol was not close. This is not just because of the traditional rivalry between Cherubim and Seraphim, but also a difference of approach. As a result of the difference between the two, Herod started a persecution of the Pharisees around the year six before the Invasion. Only by appeal to the High Command was the operation cancelled. Mardoch argued that it was known that the Pharisees would have something to do with the Messiah. Therefore, it was not opportune to send them all to hell "before their time." He insisted that it was better to have some on hand when the Messiah came than to have to look for new supposedly religious useful tools at the last minute. The Supreme Commander agreed and in this showed his usual prescience, and Mardoch later became a key player near the end of the Invasion.

The Romans were under the supervision of a cadre of officers from the Thrones, the famous Group of Five:

Orbus, Malus, Peccatus, Maculus and Depravatus. They were practiced in the art of domination by means of appetites, not only sexual—what power we have over a human who cannot control his lust! —but also Gluttony and Avarice. In fact, they used Gluttony to marvelous effect, considering the small numbers who could afford that sin. However, the Romans did not rule directly in Palestine; their subject-king Herod was really in charge. Thus, the Group of Five did not have the scope that might have made the difference in the early days of the Invasion. In terms of the actual day-to-day conduct of the war, the Roman devils were only present in an advisory status and could not do all the harm of which they were capable. Later, of course, these Five demonstrated their worth in the last phase of the Invasion when they imposed the Procurator Pontius Pilate on Palestine. He proved very useful to us. Peccatus and Maculus went on to even greater feats when they were assigned to Operation Nero, one of the finest hours of our forces, even to this date.

The Dominions were in charge of the Sadducees, although this part of the theater was also supervised by the Group of Five in some aspects. The key to the Dominion strategy with the Sadducees was Avarice. The Temple was the greatest single industry in Palestine. Rivers of money entered day by day, and most of it was controlled by the Sadducees. Their wealth, however, was based on a precarious social balance. As a social force, the Sadducees were only too aware of their dependence on Roman authority.

The Romans used them but never could get used to the difference between the Jewish priests and the more ecumenical priesthoods of the great Temples of Rome.

They considered the Sadducees bigoted and unfriendly. The representative of Rome mocked the religious customs of the Sadducees, especially when he understood that their acceptance of the Torah was not bound to a belief in eternal life. "What the hell do they do it for?" he asked famously. Their lack of professional interest in the gods of the Romans, evident on certain questions in the Temple (e.g., when the Romans wanted a statue of Jupiter placed on Temple Mount) led some Romans to consider the Sadducees atheists.

The fundamentalism of the Sadducees and their belief in finite human life made them a special case for the devils. Although it would seem to be easy to get someone to condemn himself when he doesn't believe in an eternal life, this is not always so. The Sadducees often bound themselves to ethical behavior because they felt that it would receive adequate compensation in what the earthlings call "the present life." This was what helped the Dominion gambit with Avarice. When religion is based on self-interest, it is ready-made for manipulation.

There was also the advantage of working with rich and privileged elite who absolutely detested the populace who were "below" them. Pride and Envy were subordinate strategies with them. The second was especially important with regard to the Pharisee movement. They were not jealous of the popular esteem enjoyed by the latter sect, but were aware of its commercial success. The righteousness of the Pharisees was in part the ideological apparatus with which an emerging middle class could tell an ancient aristocracy where to get off. This was, of course, gravy to us, to use an expression vaguely associated with Gluttony among humans, meaning an accidental element that invests a group of activities or materials with special savor.

The Zealots were guarded by Virtues (I see no reason to call them as some would have it, "anti-Virtues." Virtue means strength, *pace* whatever moralizing that humans have associated with the word. And our Virtues have the strength that comes from rejection of the TT). At the precise time of the Invasion, the organization of the Zealots was vestigial. There were little groups, but no leader who could gather the forces together. It was only after the death of Herod that the clandestine organization was able to increase in size and importance.

The Virtues who worked with the Zealots played to Pride and to Anger. Since Anger is passion of humans in the face of real or imagined injustice, it was easy to move from the real injustices of the Roman Imperium to a Wrath that became ever increasingly more violent. The Zealots often robbed and killed Jews in order to get funds for their guerrilla activities. Their assassinations of important Roman collaborators in the streets of Jerusalem sometimes caused panic. The rich felt it necessary to have private armies and their paranoia was fertile soil for the bad angels. The fierceness of the Zealots, their admirable *sang froid* and their absolute sense of self-righteousness (the best quality imaginable in a terrorist), were the master strokes in a minor work of art by those assigned to their condemnation.

CHAPTER TWO:
ZACHARY THE PRIEST

[This is either from a different book or is an interpolated chapter. –Informant]

There was one strange event that should have been studied more closely by the local authorities. This was concerning the priest Zachary and the birth of his son John. The pregnancy of Elizabeth, like so many others associated with prophetic figures and holy men and women, was unusual. We had almost missed the event because our agent in the Temple was trying to stir up jealousy between the priests at the precise moment Zachary was receiving his message from the other side. Priests are, among all men and women, quite prone to a spirit of competition. Perhaps only those who write are more consumed with professional envy. This has always been a great help to us, because, while hierarchs and holy men may have well-ordered lives and be quite applied to their work, they are almost to a man very much aware of perquisites and prestige.

Sometimes their idea of what prestige may mean will differ from that of the other half-clods, and include things like who can say more prayers or fast longer or make more sacrifices; there is often a genuine competition for the approbation of the laity. Thus, who could enter the Holy of Holies each year was a question of great importance for the priests in Jerusalem. It constituted a fertile field for some of our agents, who were able to sow seeds of division on the basis of the simple lottery used in the Temple to determine which priest could enter the Holy of Holies. There were always men ready to believe that the lottery was fixed, that influence had been peddled, that the really worthy had been overlooked.

Zachary's "election" had been a surprise to all factions because he really was not attached to any party or charismatic figure among the priests. For one thing, the man was too frank. He exhibited this openness even in the dialog with archenemy Gabriel in the experience in the Holy of Holies. Zachary was always raising objections to everything. That is why he was never very popular among the priests. It was inevitable perhaps that he could cavil even to an archangel in the middle of a supernatural revelation. His complaining about the impossibility of Elizabeth's conceiving was most natural for him. He always had an eye that couldn't miss the fly in the ointment, so to speak. "This couldn't happen because..." This should have worked in our favor.

While Zachary was talking to the angel, our agents were busily fanning the sparks of resentment into flame, as might be expected. *Why was he chosen? Who owed him a favor? What kind of a priest is he to enter the Holy of Holies?* This was just Standard Operating Procedure. But somehow someone lost track of the time. The man should have been in and out of the place in a minute. Instead, he was inside, and no one knew what was happening.

Partly this was because it certainly would not be possible for a devil to enter the so-called mist of the Shekinah. This was the justification used at the trial. However, there should have been more attention when the time lapse grew more considerable. Instead, our agents presumed that the man was wallowing in a unique moment in the Shekinah and used that to upset the other priests. In fact, one devil noted the thoughts of Zachary's colleagues:

Who does he think he is? This is an unconscionable amount of time. Did the incense get to the old boy? Was he talking to the Divine Presence? In which case, would we have to drag him out by his feet? What presumption for a country priest! He has no right to keep all of us waiting. Because of some kind of misguided compassion, they allow him this privilege, as an excuse not to give the opportunity to someone more worthy and less controversial, and then he abuses the moment. Has he stopped to talk to the Cherubim?

This last referred to the two carved wooden Cherubim that were the poor substitute for the brass ones that had been in the Solomonic Temple. When the Temple was shabbily rebuilt after the Babylonian Exile (another military blunder was behind that—the Persians should never have been allowed to conquer our favorite satraps in Babylon) wooden angels had been put into the Holy of Holies. Obviously, we know that the half-clods imagine us to be like them, only birdlike with great wings. What could be a cruder attempt to mock us than to say you are so special, you resemble us? The Ark was already hidden somewhere in the mountains, and will be revealed at

Armageddon, but the statues of the angels were still in the Holy of Holies. Herod had them plated with gold and it was usual for the priest on his rare opportunity to enter "That Place" to be surprised and impressed with them. Some Jews had come to believe that all images had been banned, even those mandated in the Torah, like the angels. Seeing the carved things always shook something atavistic loose in their collective unconsciousness and there had been cases of priests who almost fainted on seeing the Cherubim.

Some of the priests who had heard descriptions of the things presumed that Zachary had been overwhelmed because of what he was seeing. Something in the sight of gold and gems refracts through the senses of clay and makes it think—if you can call it that—of the so-called glory of the presence of *You Know Who*. Metals and rocks have no such joy for us, of course, but are very useful in our plans for the damnation of the half-clods, who will sometimes sell their very souls for silver and gold and diamonds and rubies. The gold-plated cedar panels in the Holy of Holies had caused feverish imagining in other priests. One had rubbed his hands over the walls in the privacy of the ceremony, as if he could take something with him of their sheen. Our agents often prepped the candidates for the Holy of Holies beforehand and had the narrow minds of the priests feverish with the vision of so much gold and envy of Zachary. Our devils were laughing with glee at how the hierarchs could be distracted so easily from their worship.

Little did the priests know that Zachary was talking to an archangel! And our own functionaries, distracted by the sinful glee of the priests, didn't know either. Obviously, entrance in the Shekinah was not an option, but the devils present might have been more attentive to the vibrations of the soul of Zachary. Another case of negligence, which demonstrates that the success of the Invasion had to do with chance phenomenon, and not as the heretical Michaelist group thinks, with an inevitable plan of rescue of the half-clods.

"Chance in a lifetime and he is mucking it up," one of the priests said under his breath. There was a buzz of response as the line was repeated down the rows of the priests in the hot sun. Several agents in place prompted the more docile priests to say to themselves and others, *"Will you come out now, you numbskull?"*

Under ordinary circumstances, this might have been useful. Unfortunately, Zachary came out wild-eyed with emotion and immediately his colleagues saw that something supernatural had happened to him. They were a cynical lot, but not without supernatural sensibility. A sense of awe washed down among the ranks of priests.

Then they discovered that Zachary had lost the power of speech. "He must have seen God," said one wag, "because only *He* could shut the man up." The atmosphere was so serious that no one laughed. Some of the priest's friends came up to him, but he was unable to communicate more than mere gestures. They all knew that something had happened, but Zachary was left to go home without even an interview with the High Priest.

The High Priest that year was one who was not overly pious, we could say. In fact, the man was too busy counting his money and plotting to get more power from the Romans to be worried about supernatural occurrences on duty. When someone hurried to the High Priest with the news that Zachary had seen an angel, he muttered, "Of course, there are two golden ones in the sanctuary."

When it was explained that perhaps Zachary had seen a real angel and maybe that he had been struck dumb, the High Priest was silent for a moment. Then he said, "Is he a Pharisee, too?" because the Pharisees were great believers in angels. The Sadducees had "risen above" that superstition. The devil who worked on that project was given the Order of Demerit.

"Not that I know of," said the priest. "If anything, some of his family had Essene connections."

"Then we must keep quiet about this. You may report that I asked whether the priest had been chosen properly and whether he had committed any irregularity before offering the incense. And that perhaps this Zachary was lucky: let them think about Nadab and Abihu and the alien fire that caused their deaths. A little fear is not without its uses for us. For all we know the man may be faking it. It was his great moment in the Shekinah. Perhaps he is hoping to make quite an impression."

The messenger, who had seen Zachary's face and felt his emotion, was shocked at the blasé attitude of the High Priest. It was the best we could do in this exchange of fire, so to speak. Zachary, as you can read in the enemy propaganda, went home to his wife in an unusual mood and as a result she conceived a son. One of our guards overheard the conversation when Elizabeth explained to Zachary that she felt different, as if something had happened to her? Could she be pregnant, she wondered, and began weeping. Zachary could not speak, but he wept also. Then he shook his head sadly, as if discounting the possibility. He knew, but he was afraid to hope for a son.

And so, he continued denying the possibility. We felt that the TT's guards were disappointed in the old man for that reason, who continued dumb.

The news was immediately communicated to the Infernal Court. His Satanic Majesty, with his usual perspicacity, immediately concluded that the conversation in the Holy of Holies had had to do with a child. It was obviously what the couple had waited for all their lives. Perhaps the old priest had prayed hoping against hope amid the gold of the sanctuary. It was a kind of test for all listening.

No action was taken because the birth of a long-awaited child of a supposedly sterile woman was an old gambit by our Adversary. It was an old trick and no one expected it to presage an Invasion.

CHAPTER THREE:
FIELD MARSHAL ABADDON

The gestation of the little prophet had caused concern, of course, among the ranks. Field Marshal Abaddon thus decided to pay a special visit to the area. It was thought, "this is not the first time a prophet has come around. There is no reason for panic." His visit was supposed to showcase the importance of the Palestinian Occupation Forces and strengthen the *esprit de corps* of the devils. His arrival in Jerusalem caused a *frisson* among all the devils. [Really, a chill? –ed.] It was supposed to be a kind of triumphal tour, showing a business-as-usual kind of style. Instead, it became a scandalous debacle. This was because of an incredibly stupid devil who had been assigned to Nazareth when he wanted to be in Jerusalem. It is not only among humans that pride causes imbeciles to think so well of themselves that they are consumed with ambition.

He was an angel by the name of Luxbel. He interrupted the famous review of the troops that Abaddon was conducting in the forecourt of the Temple to report the existence of an "almost invisible soul" and a horde of enemy agents gathered in Nazareth. His immediate superior, the supervisor of Galilee, was a Power who later transferred to the part of the world earthlings call Tasmania. His name was Mephistopheles. This Mephistopheles is famous for his part in a tragedy of Medieval Earthling times. He appears to be the object of special hatred by the Enemy, who frustrates the cleverest plans we are capable of, especially by means of exploiting human sentimentality. His rehabilitation has remained controversial in some sectors, but His Satanic Majesty is not to be questioned. Besides, Mephistopheles is famous, and what more can a devil hope for? [The Informant never commented if this Mephistopheles was the M. assigned to him. –ed.]

Luxbel interrupted the review of troops by shouting: "Invasion. The Enemy has occupied a town in the north!" There was a history to this outburst. Some earth-years before, Luxbel had informed Mephistopheles of a strange event. This involved the detection of a party of angels, mostly Thrones, which accompanied a caravan that went from Jerusalem to Ein Karem and then on to Nazareth in Galilee. On the last leg of the journey, the caravan was so heavily protected with TT troops and moved so rapidly, it had caused a small amount of discussion at staff headquarters. What were the angels up to? No logical reason for such a powerful contingent of angels could be seen. Who were these people? What was the plan for them?

Apparently, there was a file opened about the case. It moved from devil to devil until it reached Mephistopheles, who asked for more data. The caravan involved immigrants moving to Galilee from Jerusalem. Immediately, Mephistopheles drew a wrong conclusion. This was his thinking: these were people who had somehow been endangered in the Holy City. The Enemy always tends to reward his own with "spiritual consolations," as earthlings describe them.

Mephisto, as his (few) friends call him, took it that these migrants were more holy failures. The TT seems to have a definite preference for such types. And often these receive special favors, including an awareness of the divinity in their souls, but it is doubtful that it is as good as what was taken away from us.

The report included a datum that should have made the devils in charge react with dispatch. In the midst of the caravan there was a spiritual atmosphere that was insupportable. One of the devils remembered it as similar to the pillar of fire that guided Israel out of Egypt. The mystery of the painful light at the center of the caravan was puzzling, but it was thought that perhaps this was some kind of grace of compensation given to a failed prophet. Maybe some kind of rubbed-off sheen of the Shekinah was involved, like the way Moses' face shone in the desert when he talked to the Trinitarian Tyranny. That was the way Mephistopheles interpreted what Luxbel had seen and so reported it to General Ursheol, who, of course, accepted it without question. Ursheol, whose fatuity knew no bounds until he was given prison duty, did not bring the matter up with Abaddon.

Later we knew what had happened. A certain Joachim and his wife, Anna, had left Ein Karem to go to Nazareth. This was part of the secret invasion plans for Palestine concocted for *You Know Who*. Apparently, the Trinitarian Tyranny had spotted a weakness in our network of control in Galilee. First of all, the Jews themselves considered Galilee of little importance. The devils had found that prejudice among the Jews and had, in fact, helped to make it grow. In all human enterprises there is no end of evil we can make causing men to divide among themselves in groups that hate each other. Division among the Jews seemed always to be helpful. In this case, it served as a cover for very cleverly deceitful ploy on the part of the Enemy.

Secondly, there were rumors, of course, of some kind of "Divine" So-called Savior, but always the prophecies located him in connection with the city of Bethlehem. It was not logical that the attack would come at Nazareth instead of Bethlehem. Mephistopheles said in the trial, "We had trouble enough understanding why the House of David, which had become completely powerless, would have such an important part in the scheme of things, but then that *You Know Who* would change the rules on us and come in from the back door, so to speak, was never expected." The words were hollow and no one dared even to pretend to accept the argument. The reason I know of this is from an interview with Mephisto. Of course, all record of the trials has to be processed because, without censorship, how can we know the truth?

Then there was the fact that this painful light was coming from the vicinity of a young girl who was only twelve at the time of the migration from Ein Karem. "The country had too many poor girls to be worrying about each one"—those were the most unfortunate words of Luxbel at the trial. It is true that women were not being watched, even though there were clear prophecies of a young virgin bearing a child who would be the redeemer of his people.

Apparently, some of the devils in question decided to be Biblical exegetes, as certain scholarly persons are called among the mortals, and said that the correct interpretation of the passage in the prophet Isaiah was that it had to do with the Davidic dynasty in a certain point of time, specifically during the reign of Hezekiah. While this was a very good strategy to use *after* the fact of the Palestinian invasion, it was not very useful *before*. It is one thing to fool others with nonsense, another thing to begin believing it yourself.

Luxbel had been satisfied with the report and was not really concerned about the consequences. He was not the keenest observer of the miserable wretches who were assigned to Nazareth, and was more interested by the cases of strangers who moved through the town. He envied very much the devils who were assigned to the Roman Theater, because of the reach of Roman power. Who were these Jews in Nazareth? They were provincials far from power and far from being interesting, according to the benighted captain of our garrison. For that was Luxbel's rank, Captain of the Nazareth garrison. And if our officers are wretched dolts, what can we expect?

So, the guard was not vigilant and let the case go by. It was a blip on the charts, as the half-clods say. [Half-clod is a favorite diabolic expression for humans. –Informant] [Probably a reference to the composite nature of human beings, body and soul. –ed.] Nevertheless, Luxbel revisited the case because of something that was merely accidental, not to say coincidental. The devil was watching a beggar who was moving through Nazareth on his way to Jerusalem. He was a Jew from Bethlehem, Nathan by name, a slave. As a young man, Nathan had travelled far from home, got into a messy situation and eventually was sold into slavery.

There his master, a violent man, had died suddenly. Without waiting for the heirs to appear on the scene, the slave had deserted the house of his master, who had been a great merchant in Antioch. Nathan was afraid of being caught, so he dressed as a leper. This had its advantages and disadvantages. Few people wanted to get near him, so he was safer, but it also made it unlikely anyone would want to sell him food or provide lodging, either. The result was that he had a difficult time even buying bread to eat. Too clever by half is one of the half-clod expressions for a strategy like his; he wanted to avoid contact but forgot that, like all humans, he needed some sort of contact with others to survive.

He had, of course, stolen the purse of his master, who had died of a stroke while beating him. When he wandered into Nazareth, he was hungry and thirsty, and Luxbel thought he could make him desperate enough to either throw off his disguise and run amuck, or despair and decide to kill himself. There have been a multitude of such successful cases of escaped slaves driven to such despair. Obviously, this is why it represents our first option in our War Manual, but some of the incredibly stupid troops have managed to forget it at times. [Criticizing his own colleagues. Talk about no honor among thieves! –ed.]

So here he comes into Nazareth and the people run away from him. Luxbel was playing him, hoping that he could get Nathan to commit some act of violence. He did not let any of the other angels in the garrison have fun with the man. Nathan's thirst was maddening him and he shouted after some women by a well. Then, the exhaustion of days of running and poor food broke down his flesh. We can never forget how delicate these creatures are. They must constantly be feeding their material dimension and when they don't, they are hungry, and it can cause them to make decisions that they never would when satisfied.

And this can be multiplied exponentially when they ingest certain liquids containing CH_3OH, known to most of them as alcohol. It is a byproduct of natural fermentation processes, and we can all enjoy the irony. The material world decays and produces hallucinatory substances that affect the already weak will of the creatures.

Nathan then fell down in the street. Human beings have this sort of tension in them: sometimes their spirit wills to do something and their bodies fail in the execution of the same. This is an obvious result of the materials of which they are made, of course, but how many devils have forgotten that in the course of duty? I know of a case of a man about to murder his brother, who tripped on a small piece of matter and falling, began to repent his intention. The idiotic devil present on the scene did not know what to do. The game was lost.

There was Nathan in the street, cursing all who saw him and even those who didn't. He was even shedding tears. Water flows from the organs of vision of these creatures when they are emotionally upset. It is part of the complicated nature of the psychosomatic construct, and we know all the laws. However, there is a contagious character to the tears. That is what we forget sometimes. So, there he is weeping and along comes the little Miriam, coming back from the well. She rushes over to the man and gives him some water. A devil once snickered at this line, which was part of a conference I gave at the War College. It is ironic but true: humans producing water from their eyes take refreshment from a certain quantity of water poured into their bodies. A glass of water has a calming effect even on those who are sobbing.

But that bit of water was only the first part of a chain

of unfortunate events. Luxbel was stunned by the fact that a girl would help a strange man, but that, of course, is no excuse for being remiss in his duty. Then Miriam, again against all odds, helps the man to his feet. He was dressed as a leper, complete with a sort of bell on a rope around his neck. She should not have touched him. Luxbel said he thought that she did not realize the fact that the man supposedly had leprosy, but some scholars have doubted his assertion. Despite the leprosy, then, the girl helped Nathan! That should have had all the alarms going.

When Nathan was on his feet, he became afraid. Who was this girl? He obviously reacted to something in her personal characteristics, because he became very meek with her. In a whisper, he said, "I am not a leper, I am hungry," and that was enough. Miriam took him home with her and her parents attended to him. They were pious Jews; Joachim had even read the story of Tobit quite recently in the Hebrew version, which we now have managed to suppress. The solidarity they gave to the escaped slave saved his life.

There was another detail in the occurrence that alarmed Luxbel. The girl apparently had no ego, in the sense of a personal need for validation from those around her. There was no tug in her of personal pride. She did not have to resist impulses to ignore the beggar or even—on a good day for us—mock him or reject him. There was no resistance to good in her soul. That made it difficult for him to "see" her and that is why he called her invisible. She wasn't even proud of herself for being so "good."

She was "soaked to the bone" in the grace of the TT. [Interesting metaphor for a devil. I wonder about the Informant's attempts to find equivalence sometimes. –ed.]

Because of that, Luxbel turned his full attention to her. This, he said, was uncomfortable, so he focused on the periphery and that is when he was able to see the army of TT's angels surrounding the city. He had been so consumed with the drunks and prostitutes, the avaricious and the merely vicious in town that he had ignored an enormous build-up of Enemy forces.

Because direct conflict between us and the benighted angels loyal to TT has been prohibited them, apparently, we fight vicariously through human souls. The idiotic Luxbel was somehow able to ignore the myriads of angels that had arrived in Nazareth. There are always some angels present when one is dealing with human beings. Each of the half-clods, as we well know, has a kind of bodyguard angel hovering close to his ward. It must be stupefyingly boring when not humiliatingly frustrating. They are, these half-clods, so limited in scope and we angels are so far beyond them.

But this was not a case of normal custody. There were angels everywhere. The failure to see the town was practically an encampment of enemy forces was not only culpable but also stupid. [Devils have a horror of being called stupid. –Informant]

"So many angels about her and we didn't suspect anything, hey?" said the Field Marshal, and you could hear every angel thinking "uh-oh."

"We thought they were some scouts," said Luxbel.

"Oh my!" shouted the Marshal, "How clever you were to think of that. THEY THOUGHT THE ANGELS WERE SCOUTS! Of course, that made things easy, didn't it? WHAT ELSE WOULD YOU DO BUT IGNORE SCOUTS OF THE ENEMY IN ASTONISHLY GREAT NUMBERS IN A

THEATER THAT WAS ESPECIALLY SENSITIVE? I must hand it to you, gentlemen, you are indeed wonderful to my eyes."

He was being ironic, of course.

CHAPTER FOUR:
DECISION TO GO TO NAZARETH

Abaddon had expected to be amused during the fateful review of the troops, which was part of the Field Marshal's tour of Palestine. The interruption of Luxbel was annoying. But what he had said was much more than annoying. It is not an exaggeration to say that the Field Marshal was taken aback by the news. He became upset when he learned that years had gone by and he had not been told anything about the Enemy breaking through our lines. Slowly, hellishly, the details came out. His angel intelligence was alert to the fact that the Enemy would not invest a small provincial town without a strategic reason.

"And I am supposed to be thankful for your telling me this at this point in time?" said Abaddon.

"Thank you, sir," said Luxbel. Devils of angel rank have sometimes held that this response was somehow ironic, but there is no evidence of the same. The record shows it provoked some laughter.

"Who can expand on this idiot's report?" asked Abaddon.

More information was given him, as he steadily got more enraged. The girl, whose name was Miriam, was betrothed to a man much older than she, a former Essene monk, who had been born in Bethlehem.

"Bethlehem, who else was born in Bethlehem?" asked Abaddon. It was not clear whether he knew or not.

"King David," answered a devil nearby. He should have added, "The adulterous King David whom we punished by inducing his son to attempt to take away his throne and who was succeeded by another product of his lust, the lascivious and doting idolater, Solomon." That is what we had been trained to say in our preparation for the Palestinian Theater, but in the excitement of the moment, the benighted demon forgot. This shows how very small breaches of discipline can weaken the whole structure of our dominion here on Earth.

There was a flutter of energy about this.

"The monk is a descendent of David," was heard from a section of the Thrones.

"And what does that mean?" asked Abaddon. Everyone presumed that he knew, but wanted to see who had not studied history.

"It has to do with the prophecies of, you know, *the one who is to come*," said a devil, who was not known as a stutterer before that day.

"You know? I can't stand people who use that phrase as a bridge to their thought! Speak without stammering, you idiot."

Abaddon glared at the poor devil, who was assigned to work with college professors from that day. His speech was permanently affected.

"Anyone else?" shouted Abaddon.

"We have two legions of angels in Bethlehem," said Mephistopheles.

"But we are seeing a buildup in another place, no?" asked Abaddon.

"Perhaps..." Mephistopheles started to say.

"No, not perhaps. Is there anyone else with information?"

"I suppose I have," said an angel in a low voice.

"Your name," boomed Abaddon. Even among the devils there was some sympathy for the object of the Field Marshal's ire.

"Kremlin," said the poor devil. Of course, this caused more laughter.

Abaddon suddenly became avuncular with the devil, a common angel.

"They laugh at your name now, but not always. You will have a great future."

This chastened the atmosphere considerably.

"Now, what do you have to say?"

"It's about the young woman," said Kremlin. "She comes to the well where I have duty. There is something strange about her."

"What is strange?" asked Abaddon, who must have been feeling the failure of the social "event" this review in the forecourt of the Temple was supposed to have been. Some feathers of his wings were broken. [A metaphor, I suppose—God knows what this means. -Informant] He was afraid he would have to call HSM in to tell him of the strange deployment of enemy troops. "She never talks about anyone," said Kremlin, which set the other devils howling again with laughter.

Everyone expected that Abaddon would send the poor devil to the lowest corner of hell. Someone even shouted out, "And she always says grace before meals," but

Abaddon silenced the company with one look. [Whatever the Informant considered the original expression in angelic language meant. How can immaterial creatures give a "look."–ed.]

"And she is almost invisible to me. There is no contrast in her soul like in the other half-clods.

"More about this painful invisibility," groaned Abaddon. "Who can take me to see this girl? We must go, and we must inform His Satanic Majesty."

Abaddon was known for his detail work, but was also considered one of the most inclined to enjoy a party. The review of the troops in Jerusalem each year was usually a raucous success. His cancelling the games and his decision to go to Nazareth surprised some. It was, however, completely in his nature. He was an old soldier, and had caught of whiff of trouble. Without further ado, the entire company of devils departed to Nazareth, a great throng of witnesses to what would be the saddest day in our history. [This last has a human touch to it, I'm sorry to say. –ed.]

CHAPTER FIVE:
THE FIRST DAY OF THE INVASION

[This chapter also seems to be by a hand distinct from the one that wrote the others. Note the narrative "we." –ed.]

Nazareth had never seen such a gathering of spirits. The other side was there in force, so much so that some thought we were bound for Armageddon. Our camps were practically next to each other. Although we try never to have direct contact with each other, there were several times that some thought violence would break out. Those on the other side were obviously worshipping without ceasing. That made the troops of HSM tenser, because the celestial energies were swirling around the scene. I quote *in extenso* an eyewitness report of the invasion:

> At the point of contact of the two camps was a certain humble edifice, completely without luxury. In the space behind this house there was an olive tree, with leaves that seemed dipped in silver, and a mustard bush, in which some birds were singing. Someone was within the garden, but we could barely see her. Her movements were detectable, but, as a

devil had testified, there was very little contrast in her soul. The outline of the flesh was clear, but it was almost impossible for us to look at her face, which was suffused with the effusions of the power of the Enemy. This caused some consternation in the lower ranks. There was some murmuring, especially among some Thrones... [Illegible].

Suddenly, an archangel appeared. He was in human form, with enormous feathery wings. That could only mean that he wanted the human being in the garden to 'see' him. The grotesque character of this mixing with creatures made of clay offended the majority of our troops present. General Abaddon was so violently affected that he was 'doubled up in spirit' and moaned. Some thought that he was choking out the words to one of the ancient heavenly songs of praise from before the Revolution, so bad did he look and sound, and his spirit writhed in pain. It was as if he were almost worshipping against his own will. This, of course, could not be, and even to think so shows evidence of Michaelist tendencies.

The archangel, in his *quasi* human form, genuflected before the human being. She was seated on a simple stool in the garden, and he actually committed a reverence. An archangel, one of the greatest beings in the universe, curtsying before a girl, as if he were a page at the court of a princess! General Abaddon was beside himself. From the whole troop of devils, a mournful and terrible sound rose up. An archangel making reverences to a creature of clay! The howl of rage was like thunder and we could all feel its reverberations.

Then the archangel greeted the creature. He said, "Hail Miriam, the one who is full of grace, the Lord accompanies you."

The devils present immediately fell into an absolute silence. Through the whole corps of the infernal host there was felt a tremendous tension, like the arcing of a bow just before the arrow is released.

The young girl did not respond to the archangel in words. Nevertheless, her thoughts were accessible for all. She could not understand the greeting of the archangel, either. She–even she–knew that there was a terrible disproportion in an angel paying homage to a girl, and calling her "full of grace." Her surprise was unfeigned. Very clearly, we could almost hear her think, "What can this mean?"

Then the archangel said the dread words: "Miriam, do not be afraid, you have found great favor with the Most High. You will conceive and bear a son, and you will name him Jesus. This one will be great and will be known as the Son of the Most High and the Lord God will give him the throne of David his father. He should rule over the House of Jacob for all ages and his reign will never end." Dread silence captured all the troops. Some remembered the ancient rumor that divinity would dare to mix with creation. There had been angels who joined the Revolution just because of that rumor. But this was a thought so completely illogical and without respect for the order of things that some devils could not believe it.

"David his father?" The absurdity of it was what tricked us. A petty king plucked from the smelly flocks of his father to be, at the start of his public career, nothing more than a shepherd boy, then the hero who killed the giant, next the son-in-law who took the place of his bride's father and his own mentor and finally the father whose own sons sought to dethrone him: how could anyone take him seriously? He was famous, if anything, for his weakness. And then, of course, old limping Jacob had to be dragged in by Gabriel. As if rule over the house of Jacob were some great future! But of course the menace of the archangel's message lay in its deceptive simplicity. So it would be another king. Even the stuff about an everlasting reign was a cliché we had all heard before. Every petty despot in the area was supposed to reign forever. How could the archangel's words be taken as prophecy? They sounded like the usual tissue of lies human conversation represents. It had been forgotten that angels on the other side are never mendacious.

I quote from a firsthand report. "Not all the devils could understand the threat involved in the angel's words. Still, some earthly beings had been called sons of the Most High. The fact that the name of the child was "G-d saves" was not proof of anything definitive, either. Men were always saying that G-d would save them from this and that. We had nevertheless kept control of creation. The fact that the Messiah was to be the son of David we always knew. Who could worry about another earthly king? The pathetic House of David was not something we would have anxiety about. That was the attitude of some of the troops. Perhaps it was boredom, or just curiosity. They were very much interested in this interview of angel with a fleshly being, but it was not as if they had captured the horror of the moment.

Our leader of course did understand the import of Gabriel's message. No sooner did *the greeting* occur than His Satanic Majesty himself was in our midst. He knew immediately the seriousness of the threat to our occupation. He literally threw himself into the breach of the wall of darkness that separated divinity and creation. Quicker than we could imagine, he began the awful and very painful spiral turning of the spirit that is necessary in order to take on a material shape. His groans were so loud that everybody could hear him. What surprised us all is that he decided to become a snake once more."

The subtlety of our sovereign master escaped some of those who have commented on this scene. Just as he had with the interview with Eve, Satan decided upon a particular type of creature in order to infiltrate the site of the invasion. He became an asp. There were many reasons for this. Perhaps one was the fact that the devil assigned to Cleopatra, Acor, had used this disguise to such good purposes. Cleopatra was an earthly queen of a kingdom named Egypt, who, after gambling badly about lovers in a power struggle, lost everything, killing herself by clasping the small venomous serpent to her breast. Acor had made her think that suicide was the best course of action. He had done so in obvious homage to Satan, and Satan paid him the astounding compliment of replicating the gesture. There, in the garden of Nazareth, Satan took the form of an asp.

The reduction to a material form, and one that is so small as to practically go unnoticed, involved a great deal of pain for HSM. Everyone present knew what he was going through. Keep in mind that he had chosen to hide himself from an enemy. That was a humiliation he accepted in order to achieve an end. He knew Gabriel only too well. It wasn't just that he had outranked the archangel. Satan had personally appealed to Gabriel to join the Revolution. The latter's rebuff had been extremely insulting. Now Satan had to slither about the garden hoping that the archangel would not notice him. This had to be the greatest suffering for him. He would much rather have confronted the ex-friend and eternal enemy directly, of course.

I quote once more from the devil eyewitness, "We all kept silence as HSM moved gradually across the garden to where the two were talking. The daring of our great leader had some devils trembling. Satan slithered to the encounter through the wild grass and other plants. There was a moment when it looked as though a bird would interfere with the progress of HSM. We were all paying attention to the bizarre character of the encounter, but the bird got scared when it saw the open mouth of the asp. Finally, HSM drew near the feet of the young virgin. The silence in the ranks was astounding, and contrasted sharply with the voices of the other army swelling in praise and singing the celestial redundancy." [This last is a reference to the "Holy, Holy, Holy," that is the heavenly song of praise of the three persons of the Trinity. – Informant; More or less. –ed.]

Human conception outside the usual course of nature? And this child, what sort of being could he be? The Holy Spirit intervening with the pathetic creatures who were neither mud nor spirit but an awkward combination of the two!

Again, the young woman responded to the angel with an extraordinary grace. It was as if she were talking to another human being, so confidential was the tone. We could all sense both her thoughts and her words. "How can this be?" she asked, "For I do not know man."

She was more logical than the Creator. Of course, this could not be appreciated at the time, because of the howling that began to spread through the ranks. It started among the lowest ranks, but spread even to some former Thrones and Dominions. The noise caused the chorus of angels to increase *their* song in volume. It started like a symphonic poem, with all the almost infinite harmonies that the existence in heaven permits to angelic voices and eventually wrapping itself around the little house and filled the space of Nazareth up to the hills surrounding it. This was another case of the indignity of the angels who remained loyal to the Power Enthroned on High. Their praise of the absolutely most outrageous effrontery of the Divinity shows how little they think of themselves. How could they be pleased with the greatest insult of all ages? If the Divinity wanted to take up a created nature, was it not logical that the angelical nature be taken up first? This mixing of the divine with ephemeral flesh was not a reason to praise but a reason to rage against the capriciousness of the Creator. How could He love man so much? Why could His love forfeit all dignity and decorum?

The archangel continued kneeling, at least in form. "The Holy Spirit will descend upon you and the power of the Most High will overshadow you," he said. "For this reason, the child who will be born will be called Holy and the Son of God. Your cousin Elizabeth, who is now old and was thought sterile is now expecting a son. For God nothing is impossible."

Nor too *degrading*, apparently. The Son Himself to become a man. This caused a grieved silence in the ranks, a most painful one because of the momentary desperation it brought. "We were struck dumb," said an eyewitness, "Never would we have thought that Divinity would descend to a point so low."

Satan was by now at the feet of the young maid. He began to insinuate in her heart a doubt about the angel. This was not at all easy, because the swirls of the temptation stayed outside the girl like invisible smoke rings. The strategy was superb, of course. The reasoning went as follows: Maybe this was a dream. Or was this some kind of cruel hoax, a young man meant to deceive her? How could she, a simple girl, be worthy of what this messenger said? Surely this was some kind of test. She must object and say no. What did she know of kings? From what she heard, they caused more trouble than they were worth. And how would she explain that she was pregnant because an angel had told her God's power would descend over her. Her family would reject her. Joseph would be sure to expose her to the law. She would be killed. Was this something like what the Torah said about the sons of heaven and the daughters of men?

It was, of course, a virtuoso performance. No one could recapture all the ideas, impressions, half memories and feelings that Satan touched on. He tried to play on the young girl's heart as if it were a harp. And it seemed to work at first. We could all perceive her sense of puzzlement, even through the shining haze of her soul's opacity.

But there were other chords, too, of course. The

terrible hum of the angels on the other side was like the sound of a great storm approaching. But they were not the only ones who were whispering, "Yes, say yes."

The earthlings who had died before were somehow aware of the angelic interview and were speaking in Hades. We could hear their prayer, "Yes, say yes, open the door to our salvation." The sound caused consternation among some of our simpler angels. One was stupid enough to say, "Even they know." Satan did not forget the comment.

Then another sound was heard. Beginning with the birds, other creatures began to echo the refrain of the enemy. "Yes, say yes," was chirped and crowed and barked and purred throughout creation. "Redemption, redemption, redemption," murmured the leaves of the olive tree in the garden while the breeze whistled, "Yes, say yes."

We could hear the bees buzzing with it, the ants danced it, and even the fish mouthed it under water in the sea miles away. The whole restlessness and agony of enslaved creation echoed around us. It amounted to a roar of rebellion. It was a powerful reminder that we had conquered but were not loved. The clouds hissed, the melting snows insinuated it, brooks muttered it; the sea growled it; the rocks on the shore lisped it. "Yes, yes, say yes." Satan was so angry, he vowed revenge.

Of course, it was a future revenge, for at the moment he was made to suffer. He had inched his way over to the very site of the invasion. He was, in the form of the asp, at the very feet of the girl when it happened.

"I am the maidservant of the Lord; may it be done to me according to your word."

At the words, she stood up. The adjustment of her feet

in order to stand was just enough so that she managed to step on the asp. With the words there was a tremendous energy, something like a tornado of electricity, to use an earthling metaphor. The young girl was in the very vortex of the energy. That is what made her kill the asp, with the resulting suffering for Satan. It was not she; it was He in her that did it to HSM.

Obviously, an angel cannot die. The material forms we assume, however, are subject to the separation of prime matter with defining spiritual form. When that happens, there is a spiritual suffering in an angel, if nothing more than from the humiliation of the thing. The worse was that the girl did not even notice her passing triumph. She had crushed the head of the figure chosen by one of the highest creatures ever created, but she was too busy contemplating the experience of God to notice it. She was dumbfounded, as would be expected, by the wonder of a God who would forget Himself so much as to wed Himself into decaying creation.

Satan, forced out of the dead skin of the snake, reeled and reeled in another kind of tornado that swept up many of the devils. He growled and then screamed as he backed away from Nazareth toward the wilderness. All the devils howled with him and retired to the desert to parley.

CHAPTER SIX:
THE SHOW TRIAL

[Historical framing of the next phase of resistance and the edited transcripts from the trial of Luxbel and Mephistopheles. The trial of Ursheol is guarded by a thousand devilish traps and I was unable to download it, even in angelic. All that I could glean about it was a few references. –Informant]

The retreat to the desert was only tactical. The devils had to have their due, however, and so there were court-martials. This helped cheer the troops up considerably. A good show trial can do much for *esprit de corps*. Once the howling stopped, the tribunal about who made the mistakes that led to the allowing of the Virginal Conception and subsequent birth began in serious.

Because of respect for the chain of command, those investigated were Abaddon, Ursheol, Mephistopheles and Luxbel. Abaddon, who is one of the great survivors, was eventually rehabilitated and has even been chosen for the High Command, but at first he was transferred to Antarctica to the Institute of Higher Strategy.

Ursheol, of course, could not offer any explanation of

his conduct. His subordinates had let him down, but that was something we are taught to expect. (It is straight from the Manual: "Do not trust anyone to do evil, not even yourself. Constant vigilance!") Even those who had been his guests for the famous games of the capital sins thundered "Idiot" when he tried to say that he had thought that the really important things were happening in the royal court and not in simple villages among simple people. The shout was taken up so that all hell vibrated with the staccato, "Idiot, Idiot, Idiot." The lower rank devils took up the chant with a mixture of glee and *mauvaise foi*. [The Informant thought it reasonable that devils would use key phrases from French Existentialists. –ed.]

The Transcripts

[Heavily edited, like when the FBI releases documents they would rather not. The transcripts read like those from the show trials in the Gulag Archipelago. Ursheol and Mephistopheles must have been rehabilitated because the only transcripts treat of Luxbel's case. –Informant.]

Prosecutor: If it please the court, we will introduce our first accused, Luxbel.

HSM: Bring the idiot forward. [At least there was no pretense of neutrality, I suppose, not like some of our judges. –ed.]

Prosecutor: We have before us a sad example of a functionary of our regime who was not worthy of the trust accorded him putting him in charge of Nazareth.

Luxbel: (Laughter, quickly suppressed.)

HSM: Do I hear laughter?

Luxbel: I thought it was satire. Even the Jews don't like Nazareth. Worthy of the trust is such a, such a...

Thunderclaps

Luxbel: I am very sorry for my interruption of the prosecution with an outrageous series of hiccups that were reasonably construed to be laughter, but weren't, because I am cognizant of my entire blame in the case, shared, of course, with some others.

Prosecutor: I shall proceed. First point in the scandalous negligence of Luxbel was the ignoring of the family of the girl Miriam, their special history, the obvious sycophantic devotion they had to the Trinitarian Tyranny...

Luxbel: I was sent for sinners, wasn't I? Not the minority who were poor and lived lives of desperate piety.

More thunderclaps.

Luxbel: Somehow my words did not reflect my deep consciousness of terrible guilt. I beg the court's pardon.

Prosecutor: Secondly, Luxbel and company did not have prudence in dealing with unusual circumstances.

Luxbel: Prudence! I thought we hated prudence. That's you, too, Mephistopheles; don't look like you're not in on this.

Prosecutor: There will be no communication with co-defendants, even the kind of leering smear attempted by the last remark.

Luxbel: Just saying. I beg a thousand pardons of HSM and his court.

Prosecutor: No investigation was made of the fiancé of the girl in question. He was of the Davidic line...

Luxbel: Mephisto can help me here. You see, the literalism of the Davidic mystique, let's say, if not a mistake—that's a joke, by the way, you know, "mystaque"—

is debatable. The question was controversial, and it has been the subject of much argument among devilish scholars. When I was in periodic re-education camp, most devils who were scholars told us that the Davidic descent of the Messiah was not going to be literally a question of family ties to King David. It was a poetic thing, a mythic trope. Allow me the position that the Davidic line was less than impressive, even humanly speaking, which is saying a great deal. At the present time, not one of the descendants of the awful King David can be found in a position of influence in Israel. The family lines in fact became very blurred.

Prosecutor: If it please the court, I wish to call as witness the Throne who has studied the question, Mer-schu.

HSM: Let him be brief. [Like he knew what was coming. –Informant]

Prosecutor: Of course, Highness.

Witness was brought forward.

Prosecutor: As regards Joseph, the fiancé of the young woman in question. Can you tell me any details about him?

Luxbel: Objection, too broad.

HSM: What the hell do you know about it to be objecting. What do you mean by "too broad?"

Luxbel: I have looked into the future and that is an objection used sometimes in the best of trials.

HSM: I would warn you of looking into the future, especially television. You have enough mistakes in the moment.

Luxbel: Of course. My apologies.

Prosecutor: Angel Mer-schu? About the fiancé.

Mer-schu: Yes, the man in question was an Essene monk who left the monastery suddenly. It was rumored that he was to be involved in the Galilean revolt against Roman authority led by a certain Judas. There was a group working on getting the Essenes to get involved in the [incomprehensible], er insurrection of said Judas. [Mentioned in Acts 5:37, not the Freudian slip, of course. –ed.] It is possible that Joseph was sent to Nazareth to communicate with the Zealot movement and then was swept into another plan involving the young woman.

Prosecutor: Was this Joseph of the House of David?

Mer-schu: As I refer in my doctoral thesis [Of course devils have Ph.Ds. –ed.] *The Davidic Dynasty Down at its Heels*, there were several groups of individuals in Palestine that could claim descent from the person in question.

Prosecutor: You mean King David?

Mer-schu: Of course. Who else would it be?

Prosecutor: Yes, and the theory that the Davidic promise was some kind of mythopoeic expression? [Of course the devils would use the phrase "mythopoeic expression"! –ed.]

Luxbel: Objection. Unfair characterization. There was good reason to doubt that the prophecies about the Messiah and the house of David are meant to be taken literally as a plan by the Enemy. It is certainly more likely that he would not limit the scope of our vigilance by eliminating all of the people who did not descend from the king. Only an earthling would think that one particular family of these Jews would have some *exclusive* rights connected with the coming of the Messianic individual.

Thunderclap.

Prosecutor: Your highness?

HSM: One more stupid objection framed as a plagiarism from absurd television shows like that and your chances of receiving a pardon are lost for a million half-clod years.

Luxbel: Is the world going to last that long?

HSM: Shut up, already.

Prosecutor: Mer-schu? Your opinion of the mythopoeic interpretation of the Davidic promise?

Mer-schu: Not worth responding to.

Prosecutor: I beg your pardon?

Mer-schu: Not worth a dam.

Prosecutor: Do you care to rephrase that?

Mer-schu: No.

Prosecutor: I really wish you did. That word...

HSM: Idiot, he referred to "dam" the Indian coin! Carry on.

Luxbel: D-A-M means an Indian coin of little value? What about the expression the Devil and his Dam?

Thunderclap.

HSM: Don't make me come down from this bench, Luxbel. Only half-clods have mothers! Since you are such a good speller, try this. D-U-M-B.

Luxbel: My point precisely.

Thunderclap.

Luxbel: Just trying to clarify things.

Mer-schu: I thought I was here to establish dynastic link between said Joseph and House of David.

Prosecutor: Well, yes, but I would like to establish my case logically. You are only supposed to answer my questions.

Luxbel: I guess I am not the only one addicted to those lawyer shows.

HSM: Enough fluff, get to the question!

There was a pause before the court could get back to work.

Prosecutor: Of course. Regarding the connection between Joseph and the House of David...

Mer-schu: Yes, the monk is a descendant of David. We have the twenty-eight generations right on hand. David begat Solomon—although I am glad to point out that the mother was an adulteress who had married her husband's murderer—Solomon begat Rehoboam, Rehoboam begat Abijah, Abijah begat Asaph...

Prosecutor: There seems to be no need...

Mer-schu: Asaph begat Jehoshaphat, Jehoshaphat begat Joram—

HSM: Enough!

But the poor devil who had done the research did not even listen to what HSM was saying. The rest of the devils were listening with the hope that there would be some mistake in the genealogy.

Mer-schu: Joram begat Uzziah...

A lightning bolt interrupted the genealogy and the resounding vibration astounded the devils in attendance. For a moment there was dead silence. Theories about the reaction vary. Some say that the listing of ancestors had been an excruciating way of coming to awareness that things had gone terribly wrong.

Prosecutor: So, there is no question that the man is of royal blood?

Luxbel: Objection, leading.

HSM: What did I tell you about objections?

Luxbel: That I should not repeat another absurd objection like the future dramas that will be the intellectual pabulum of the bourgeois some centuries hence. I thought this one was logical.

HSM: I didn't say whatever you just said.

Luxbel: But you implied it.

HSM: Are you telling me what I implied?

Luxbel: Of course not.

HSM: Prosecutor, finish your questioning! This is starting to sound like a Congressional hearing. Let's save that ____ for them. [Censored by me. It's worse than you think. –Informant]

Prosecutor: Regarding the young woman? Is there any evidence of Davidic descent?

Mer-schu: This Miriam, espoused to this Joseph, begotten by—

HSM: Ya **basta!**

End of transcript.

CHAPTER SEVEN: APPENDICES OF TRIAL OF LUXBEL, ETC.

Appendix One: Historical Background

Printed like in a textbook: [Apparently some kind of written testimony that may or may not have been used at the trial. –Informant.]

A little historical background should not be necessary, but I will give it anyway. The kingdom of Israel had been restored to being in part thanks to the cleverness of the Idumean King Herod. The Maccabees had not been kings, but high priests. When their dynasty came to its bloody end, Antipater the Idumean came to the fore. Enter the delightful family: Antipater's son and heirs. Herod was one of our great "survivors" in history. His father was assassinated because he had backed those who killed Julius Caesar. Nevertheless, Herod was able to get the Roman Senate to elect him "King of the Jews" and became a "friend" of the emperor Augustus. He changed what had been a theocracy into a monarchy.

The Herodian dynasty was ideal for our purposes. It was hated by all sides, but at the same time violently repressive, a formula always attractive for us. Unfortunately, it was doomed to failure. The prejudices of the Jews, which in some respects were useful to us, militated against the Herodian gambit. Even though Herod called himself basileus, *"king," the people "knew" that the only legitimate kings for them would be of the house of David. This had been the stumbling block of the Hasmoneans, the so-called Maccabees, also. The Enemy has sometimes used the collective ignorance and prejudice of the people as a tool. No one at the time of the Invasion would have been able to give philosophical or theological criteria for legitimacy in power among the people of the Covenant. However, the poorest and most uneducated could say, "but the king should be the son of David."*

This literalism meant that our attempts to make the sovereignty of the nation somehow independent of the Davidic line would be ultimately unsuccessful. It was bruited about by some of those under our influence that the Messiah-ship was something to be applied to the people collectively. The promise of the Messiah was really about the whole nation. The personal attributes of a supposed savior of the nation were nothing else but a poetic expression of what would happen for the people. A group and not an individual would fulfill the Messianic expectations. "Depersonalize goodness whenever possible, personalize evil as much as possible" is, after all, one of the cardinal principles of the Book of Strategy that we all live by.

Some of the Zealots were ready for this theory that was so subtle that it was congruent to our subtle devilish intelligence. But it was a case of being too clever by half. [Whatever that means in the context. –ed.] *Certainly, the theory has become useful in subsequent centuries. But what serves now did not serve then. The whole thing, the Zealot theory, the guerrilla movement that seemed so important, was a dangerous trap, as events demonstrated. Once again, the Enemy stooped to conquer. By means of an unnecessary literalism, he caught us completely by surprise.*

Appendix Two: Some notes on the trial

[Mephistopheles' trial was expunged from the records; however, an analysis appended to the trial transcripts gives some conclusions that refer to Mephistopheles' testimony. It is hard to tell what the hell was going on. - Informant. I guess this is what passes for humor from our poor man's Faust. -ed.]

Luxbel had been, intellectually, like all of those in the Palestinian theater, ready for the eventual attempt to raise up an insurrection against our rule with a so-called Messiah. He was not prepared for the sneaky intervention of the Enemy in our territory. Saturating someone with grace like what was done to the girl was a new low for the TT, so we can understand why it puzzled an agent like Luxbel. Nevertheless, he was culpably guilty of lack of due diligence. [Naturally the devils speak legalese. -Informant] We must never forget how crafty our Opponent is. His very ingenuousness is really disingenuous.

So, several very important details were ignored:

One was the question of the ties of the young girl to the Davidic house. The specifics are seen in the third narrative of the Palestine Invasion that earthlings read so assiduously, the work of a Greek physician (not even a Jew, just one of those sympathizers that have abounded so much through history) named Luke. The genealogy presented by said physician ties the mother of *You Know Who, Jr.* to the Davidic line, also. But this was like the presence of an object missed by the pulses of high frequency electromagnetic waves and thus was not reflected back to the source [This is apparently a devil's joke giving the scientific definition of something coming under the radar. –Informant] as some of the benighted creatures say, because the Jews only counted descent in the male line. The unusual datum is that Matthew, the first canonical narrative, has one list of ancestors, and Luke the third, has another. We have since used this to good stead, trying to make the half-clods conclude that neither genealogy is correct, but that was a much later strategy. Luxbel could have established the so-called invisible girl's genealogy if he had tried. Ineptly, idiotically, he did not.

Another great error was forgetting about adoption and inheritance. "Since these were human realities," said Mephistopheles in the trial, "they were very difficult for us to control." He was not asked to change the laws about adoption. He was to understand that any infant born of the girl would have carried on the ancestral house of his supposed father. Thus, the baby born of the virgin Miriam, who was espoused of a certain Joseph, a bizarrely unpretentious offshoot of a family of kings and sinners, would automatically be considered "of the house of David." That should have been part of the standard operating procedure for agents in all of Palestine. Anyone who in any way was associated with the House of David should have been under surveillance.

Later, Luxbel would say that his testimony in the trial had been riddled with "unfortunate phrasing." He was made to sign his Admission of Guilt by pulling a feather out of his own wings. [This last turn of phrase seems difficult for me to accept because angels, even fallen ones, are completely spiritual beings without material attributes. However, I suppose that our Informant was trying to express some especially difficult kind of infernal metaphor. –ed.]

There had to be other signs in Nazareth that were suspicious, but all were ignored. The history of Joachim should have been a red flag for us. [The Informant's colloquial style is often reflected in the prose of the devils. Often, it makes them sound American. I am not sure what to attribute this to. –ed.] The holiness of the mother of the girl would have been another. The idyllic life they lived, etc. All had been ignored while Luxbel had fun with town drunks and loose women.

In some ways, Luxbel's failure was emblematic of our colonial regime in Palestine. Certainly, Mephisto's part in this should not be ignored. He was Luxbel's superior and like him concentrated so much on the sinners that he neglected the saints. "But we can't control them, can we?" Mephistopheles asked at the trial, and then "Even their weak wills are still free, aren't they? Human realities are in the final analysis beyond our control."

HSM hates clichés like "in the final analysis." "Not to control but to subvert and pervert human realities is why you were stationed in Palestine, you foolish oaf," the Satanic Majesty shouted to Mephisto at the court martial, which caused much uproarious laughter on the part of the other devils present. Mephistopheles was caught out, of course, and what could be more humiliating than making half of hell scream in laughter at you? There is in this a lesson for all of us not to displease HSM with frivolous excuses for our damnable stupidities.

So, the Enemy had outflanked us by sending the family of the girl to the sticks. [Again, a question of translation? –ed.] "Satanic Mindfulness" would require that every detail of any part of Palestine, every person, domestic animal and non- domestic, every tree, every blade of grass be under suspicion, guilty, until proven innocuous. So Luxbel had noticed the mysterious transfer of one poor refugee family and had routinely reported it, perhaps lacking anything to write to the superiors about. But he certainly had not conveyed any sense of urgency until it was too late. The poverty of the family of Joachim and Anne was not an excuse to ignore them. Our Opponent has often used the most miserable of half-clod beings on offer to work that Will which we will fight to our final victory, Hail Satan, etc.

This is not to deny the baseness of the Enemy's tactics. The movers and the shakers of the time were from powerful families whom we have been watching and even, in a few cases, promoting, for years. They had wealth, great houses in Jerusalem, a certain position vis-à-vis the society of their times. No one expected a poor couple and their small child would be any threat.

"I never thought such miserable wretches would have something to do with an invasion," said Luxbel at his turn in the dock at the show trial.

"Well said, you yourself are a miserable wretch; you damn yourself as a useless dunce," shouted Mephistopheles from the bench of the accused. This was later taken as a mitigating factor in his own sentence. The correctness of a superior calling one of his subjects a "damned fool" has later become a subject of discussion in some sectors. The official interpretation was that the humiliating insult constituted a contribution to the trial, an expression *bien trouvé,* or whatever. [I'm not sure this was not just the Informant's "whatever," although the word has diabolical echoes. –ed.]

To summarize the defense of the parties involved: The location was absurd, the suspicious person was the wrong sex, and the family was the wrong kind of family. But perhaps the real reason was that the daughter had some kind of special protection from our detection mechanisms. What Mephistopheles and Luxbel should have done was to have referred the cases to their superiors or even HSM. Something was wrong with the caravan? Then it should have been reported. The transfer of personnel would have given us a better chance of predicting the invasion, at least in some aspects.

This is more a scholarly point, but perhaps worth noting. [sic –ed.] Why does it seem that we can do more than the so-called "good" angels can? Obviously, their "respect" of human freedom is a great handicap. We do not "respect" it, but try to turn it to our advantage. Other scholars say that it is because of the primordial disloyalty of the human race. The sin of the first people has been passed on like some kind of congenital disorder. Without tremendous transfusions of grace, the half-clods can really do nothing right. There are some who say that it requires much more effort for the humans to do something right than it is for them to do wrong things. Certainly, it seems so at times, but we should not count on victory in each case. The player who comes on the field expecting to win easily is often defeated. [This is another example of the manuscript that makes one wish to know the original language and how sports metaphors find their way into the translation. –ed.]

CHAPTER EIGHT:
COMMANDER NECANS

[The narrative seems to have suffered substantial deletions. –Informant. Whoever wrote this chapter is a wag. –ed.]

The trials were over. Ursheol was consigned to one of the lowest levels of hell, and that seemed to help pick everyone's spirit up a bit. In a later time one of our great allies said of a world power that occasionally one of the admirals of the fleet had to be hanged, "*pour encourager les autres.*" [To encourage the others, naturally the devil would like Voltaire. –ed]

Now, there was work to be done. There was the great question of what to do. It became the subject of an official government inquiry. Satan said he wanted to hear the ideas of the demonic assembly, that he was open to hearing creative solutions from the best minds. Because no one was sure what answer was desired, there was certain reluctance among the devils to risk taking a position. Most of them were waiting for more "information," wet fingers in the wind to see which way it blew. [Again, translation or paraphrase? –ed.]

"I want creativity," HSM said. The concept was not immediately understood by the upper echelons. Finally, Abaddon took up the task of asking the members of the Security Council one by one. There was a general shudder in the upper ranks, while the lowest devils seemed to be relieved. A small group of angels even took up the mantra, "Creativity, Creativity, Creativity," until a Throne shouted them down. [Apparently few devils have the sheer rage of the Thrones who gave up adoration of God Himself on His throne to attend Satan and his vulgar caprices. Their frustration at no longer adoring makes them the cruelest of the lost angels. –Informant]

"I would have Herod order the mass destruction of Nazareth," said the first member of the Security Council.

"Would you like to go to the last corner of Hell and talk the ideas over with Ursheol?" asked HSM.

This intervention caused some laughter.

"Well, no," said the poor devil.

"Then why don't you just refrain from incriminating yourself any further. Let me pick another one of these great minds," continued Abaddon, who could see that the hard line was the right tack to take. Satan himself laughed. His laughter is unmistakable, of course. [This sounds like a terrible hacking cough, whose violence I heard once on a digital recording. Not a nice sound. –Informant]

"Maybe we could stir up an Egyptian attack on Palestine," asked a devil who had a hard time keeping historical periods straight.

"And why should they attack Palestine?" asked Abaddon in a tone that did not show the tremendous irony that was behind the question.

"Old rivalries, memories of the Ten Plagues...er, I

mean, that there is a historic enmity between the countries."

"Indeed. Here is something remarkable, comrades. An angel with almost human intelligence. May I ask where you are presently assigned?"

"I have been in charge of the market ladies in Tyre," the angel answered in a voice so unenergetic that many of the common devils could not hear him. Some of these began rumbling, "Answer the question, answer the question, answer the question," until a grunting sound from HSM himself had to intervene. The silence that followed put a pall on Abaddon's specific line of questions.

"It is a shame to waste such talent," said His Satanic Majesty, "I think that the poor devil could profit from an experience on the internal front, as I call the last circle of hell. Instead of making the market ladies sin, he has apparently adopted both their type of human reasoning and their well-known acquaintance with the world. Egypt, Idiot, is not an independent country now and is under Roman sway. Go back to making the ladies put wax on the bottom of their scales in order to cheat customers by a few ounces, and don't ever again offer advice to this Council."

"It wasn't advice, sir, I was asked a question." This last bit was offered in the hope that the greater audience of the tribunal would sympathize with him. Nothing could have been further from that than the reaction it caused. No devil likes a loser, especially one who admits it. This is especially the case where there is a need for assigning guilt. His predicament caused howls of infernal laughter to reverberate in the desert trial scene.

Five devils later, a new idea was heard.

Mara spoke. He was greatly respected because of what

he has been known to do in what the humans quaintly call the Far East. A sphere can hardly have east and west, mind you, but that is how the half-clod mind works.

"I think that we should move through the fellow who is supposed to marry the girl."

This caused another wave of commentary. Most of the devils had neglected to remember that the girl had an intended.

"I suggest that he be tempted to expose her."

There was another *frisson* in the assembly [Devils and chills, again. –ed.], almost as if angels could have something like an earthling emotion. Most saw the merit of the suggestion, even while trying to think why something so obvious had escaped them.

"And how to you intend to do this?" Satan was really quite stentorian. It is said that he frightened several small devils back to the inner circles of hell by this question. They thought that it meant that he was displeased. On the contrary, His Satanic Majesty was most intrigued with the idea.

"I suggest that I and Belphegor [Typical diabolic grammar: *not* "Belphegor and I." –Informant] go down and tempt the old fellow with two of the most wickedly beautiful women to hit the caravan trail. Belphegor really does a great impression of a lady of the night, and I can give him ideas when he runs out of them."

This was well received, because Satan chuckled. [Sounds like a smoker's dry cough. –Informant] This allowed the entire assembly to let out some of its stress. It seemed like the best possible idea. Several devils started to sing the song the prostitutes of Baal sang at their temples.

Then suddenly, someone else spoke.

Necans was a Power; it was rumored that he had had second thoughts about the rebellion a few microseconds before it had happened. Then he made the supreme effort to resist his cowardice and subservience to *We All Know Who*, and joined the rebellion. Satan appreciated what he brought to the cause and even seemed to give him more liberty than others of the General Staff. He had conquered his wretched inclination to subservience to WAKW in more ways than one. [Acronym for We All Know Who. – ed.]

"I think that Commander Mara should think again what type of man we are dealing with. Your reasoning is *meretricious*, to say the least. [Putting on the dog, the devil is, with the fancy words. –ed.] How can we ignore the fact that this Joseph is an Essene? It is true that he left the monastery, but not because he thought that it was too hard. On the contrary, he apparently believed that it was not hard enough in the desert. He decided that he had to try to purify himself in the world. This man is not likely to mix it up with the girls from the caravan. Nor is he likely to sin freely. He is a man of tremendous discipline, truly a rare human being. Why would you think that he would stoop so low as to let a *putana* make him expose his intended?"

Necans always spoke with a great authority. Already some of the devils were taking his side. There is no easier way into a devil's heart than to expose another for a fool. Satan himself obviously took very seriously Necans' objections. Mara and Belphegor were silent. This silence revealed their tacit acceptance of the other's reasoning.

Finally, Mara blurted out, "And so how would you get the work done, brother?"

This is a tremendous insult for a devil for obvious reasons. What could be more hateful to us than to be compared to the half-clods, who share something with other sons and daughters of their progenitors? We are after all free of what the idiots call family. The other was quick to respond to it.

Necans was not having any of it.

"Comparing us to human children? Do you think that I am the only one insulted by the comparison? You would be the other sibling—you idiot! If you want to reject my idea, do so. But let us not go calling each other 'brother.'"

This had caused a raucous laughter among certain ranks. There is always some fun among devils when the word idiot is tossed around. In fact, the insult was quite inappropriate and even oxymoronic. An insult (calling a spirit "brother") should not be a two-edged sword slicing the insulter also.

Satan once again called for order, this time with a volcanic explosion of wrath.

"You idiots! There is nothing funny about this!" cried HSM.

This outburst again frightened some of the poor devils, and even some Principalities looked nervous.

"Tell us what you recommend, Necans," seethed Satan. The sound was like that which would be made by a gigantic serpent, large enough to swallow the earth. [How this was in the original bewilders me. –ed.]

"I am happy to do so, Your Majesty," said Necans in a tone of voice that another devil would not have dared to use. "The man must expose the woman to the Jewish law, which considers the transgression of espousal as adultery. We all know what they do with adulterers. That has given us all some enjoyable moments. Nothing should be easier than to convince the man to expose her. I would find the village gossip and make it interesting to that person to put pressure on Joseph.

"This person would use his religious faith *for* us instead of against us. The woman in question would suffer the fate of some of her 'sisters,' and the child she has conceived will die with her." Necans' accent gave such emphasis to the words that a thrill passed through the assembled devils.

The plan was accepted and Necans immediately went to work.

CHAPTER NINE:
THE UN-MERRY WIDOW

[Whoever the devil wrote this was a frustrated novelist. – ed.]

Esther was a widow in Nazareth, a very unhappy one. She was, besides, a wealthy one, because the inn that she and her husband had managed had been able to expand its business in recent years. She had been able to purchase horses to be sold or traded to travelers in a hurry. These made a good profit and it was unlikely her customers would ever pass by again, which meant that she did not have to worry too much about the quality of horse she had on offer. Because she was a shrewd person, her employees were afraid of her. They would never allow her to be cheated by others and were loyal to her reputed capacity. Among the half-clods one is valued not for what one is but what others suppose one to be.

She had had her sights set on Joseph from the first day he arrived in town. He appeared to be a good man and she had a personal repugnance to the idea of a man, especially a good one, living alone. It was not right; it offended nature. Of course, she had heard about the religious group, the Essenes, living on the edge of the desert, whose members lived chaste lives, but she had never been impressed with what she had heard about them. Perhaps in her heart of hearts she was a bit of a Sadducee. She believed in this life, and, although she would never admit being skeptical about eternal life, she was secretly doubtful about it.

Necans visited her in the character of a wealthy relative of Joachim, the father of Miriam, who was supposedly passing through Nazareth. He insinuated that he was rather shocked about the intended marriage with Joseph. He also asked very pointedly whether Esther ever heard anything strange about "little Miriam." Esther had known about Joseph's proposed marriage to Miriam and naturally had been opposed to it. She had seen the whole thing for what it was: a scheme of Anne, "the mother," to take care of her only daughter. The girl was not a suitable mate for Joseph. He needed a more mature woman.

In fact, because of her personal interest in the case, Esther could not understand the motivation of the union between the carpenter and the young girl. She suspected that the girl's parents had somehow enticed him into it. Joseph no doubt had respect for them, whoever they were. She did not really know Joachim and Anna because they were also from someplace else—she did not really remember where, she presumed it was near Jerusalem. Some people had hinted that they were from an important family in Judea that even had some priestly ties but had fallen on hard times.

That might have been the bond between them and the strange silent carpenter, but Esther could not really understand anything that could not be counted and stored in the vault. She had heard that somehow this Joseph had met the couple and their daughter his first week in Nazareth. Immediately, he began taking his meals with them, for which he paid. The same was the case for laundering his clothes. Anne and her daughter washed them to supplement their meager household income. A single man could do nothing else than pay for what a wife would do. What was he to eat? What was he to wear?

However, Esther had offered another option. When he worked for her briefly on some carpentry in her house, she had invited him to take his meals on the job. This he had refused for what she assumed were religious reasons. Then she had offered him a job at the inn as a kind of handyman. There was always work for someone who had many different skills, and Joseph was a tremendously focused worker. He had no interest in the inn, he said, he wanted to set up his own shop. She had been nonplussed for one of the few times in her life, and he had gone on to work for himself. Although she had found reason to commission various works from him, including a chest for her coins, he had managed to elude her always. It seemed that he only came to see her when she sent a servant to ask about a specific work project. Never was she able to have him all to herself. She had practically resigned herself to the loss of the man who had attracted her attention, when things got interesting again.

What Necans said about rumors made Esther investigate the case more thoroughly. "Scratch a little, you will be surprised at how much turns up," she had said to herself, "Just like a mother hen." Very soon, Esther was aware that "little Miriam" had fainted at the well. Three women thought that she looked plumper than she had before and that her cheeks were rosier. They had heard of the espousal and therefore needed little prompting to think the worst of the girl's situation. Another suggested that Joseph was not such an Essene as all that.

She sent one of her stable boys to talk to Joseph. He was to bluntly accuse the man of having anticipated his relations with the girl. This he could insinuate in the way he knew best. What worried her was that maybe Joseph was, indeed, the father of the child. Esther felt sure Miriam was pregnant. She hoped that Joseph was not the father, because that would complicate her plans. If he were not the father, then he was playing a cuckold even before getting to the marriage bed. For a religious person, she saw this as appalling, but it suited her purposes exactly. Earthlings have this wonderful capacity of invoking religious principles when it suits them; it is one of our many aces in the hole. [I presume this is an approximate rendering of some angelic metaphor. –ed.]

Those people had come from Jerusalem (that is how Esther thought about Joachim and Anne, for she did not know about Ein Karem) and had not mixed with others because they considered themselves too good for little Nazareth. And now this—a young girl pregnant and promised to a mature man. But such scandalous deeds would not be tolerated.

Jacob, the stable boy Esther sent to investigate, did not understand much of this, but he was able to gather that, if there really was a pregnancy, then Joseph was not aware of it. He duly reported what he had conjectured to his mistress, whose interest in the case intrigued Jacob. Why was the old lady so interested in the case? He decided that the old bag was jealous, which was a correct conclusion in the case. Esther drank in the news like a camel that has marched four days through the desert drinks water from a sweet well. So, Joseph did not know what half the town knew, or so thought Esther. Joseph's ignorance made Esther go to look at Miriam for herself. She went to the house under the pretext of searching for a new servant girl. What she needed, she said, was company. She would help the girl prepare for her marriage, but she understood that that was not proximate. The girl could learn a little bit around Esther's business.

Anne told her that the girl was going to marry soon. Besides, they were going to send her to take care of a relative who was expecting a child. As soon as they were sure of a caravan down to Judea, Miriam was going to leave. That would be a few months. Esther felt frustrated with the visit, but begged Anne at least to be able to greet the young girl. She would have a gift for her wedding, she announced. When the girl was brought out to her, Esther was convinced that she was pregnant. Some earthlings have infallible instincts for what they consider scandal. Necans had chosen his player well. She knew exactly what to do.

Her next step was to visit Rachel, the wife of the synagogue leader. Esther knew that Rachel's husband, Ruben, was a most uxorious man, completely under Rachel's thumb. He listened to Rachel in everything but the interpretation of the Torah, and even then would not dare say something his wife would criticize him for. He knew Joseph very well because the carpenter came to prayer and studied the Torah on the Sabbath.

"You know I don't usually talk about people," said Esther.

"Of course," said Rachel. The two women would not have been friends if they did not gossip, but that is part of the natural hypocrisy of humans. They can deny a vice even while in the midst of its practice. Their lack of honesty to themselves is something we can never really understand—we are too smart for that. [This kind of demonic sententiousness is quite typical of the narrative. For that reason, I have only transcribed exemplary comments. If not, we would have a manuscript riddled with insults about human nature and its fallibility, a topic that delights the devils. –Informant]

"Well, there is something unusual going on about little Miriam and Joseph the carpenter."

"Don't tell me," said Rachel. That always means, "Please don't make me beg you tell someone else's secret" in human parlance.

"There is a strange rumor that she is..."

"Pregnant!" shouted Rachel so loudly that her servant girl found it necessary to leave off working in the garden to sweep in the corridor just outside of the room where the two grand dames were talking. The famous curiosity of humans is often their downfall and our best ally.

"I am afraid so, but that is obviously not the strangest part. It is that Joseph doesn't or didn't know. Actually, he *couldn't* know." Esther said all this for the maximum effect on Rachel, who had to cover her mouth again not to scream.

"How do *you* know?"

"A guest at the inn. He didn't really tell me everything, but I gathered that he was not happy with what the two old people were doing to the carpenter. I sent one of my workers to investigate a bit."

"I must tell Ruben," said Rachel.

"Do you think it wise?" Esther was playing a game with the other. Not being intelligent does not prevent humans from trying to trick each other. And succeeding, too.

"It is an offense against justice. You know the poor man seems to have drifted here from out of the desert, but he does not deserve to be treated that way. I know there are rumors about him and those monks, but I have always felt sorry for him. He needs someone like you, Esther, to make him a home and a normal life."

"I am too old," said Esther, thinking, "Oh no, I'm not! Of course, you're right."

"He is no young thing, either," said Rachel. "You both deserve a normal life."

CHAPTER TEN:
SUSPICION FAILS

[Much clearer devilish point of view. –ed.]

Soon after the visit Esther paid to Rachel, the latter found her way to the well in the early morning for her own look at little Miriam. She was also convinced immediately that something very wrong was about to happen. Earthlings have certain intuitions that are hard to explain. There is a way of knowing they have that we cannot always grasp. They are made of mud, but somehow reverberations of things enter into their consciousness by means of some kind of a filter. [The agent intellect of the Thomists? –ed.] It did not take Rachel very long to let Ruben know that Joseph was being mocked in the cruelest of tricks.

The topic became an obsessive one for the couple. Ruben thought that it was better to let things run their course. That, of course, was his attitude toward nearly everything. Rachel would hear none of this. She knew that Ruben had to do something. What did it mean to be leader of the synagogue if it was not to intervene in circumstances that appeared to her as catastrophic? The discussion heated up and finally Rachel presented her husband with an ultimatum. Either he would do something, or she would have Joseph come to them and she would confront the man herself. "The truth is truth," she said. This threat led Ruben to ask Joseph to talk to him privately after a Sabbath service.

"This girl you were intending to marry, are you aware of what has happened to her?" Ruben had no way of coming to a subject gradually.

"I don't know what you mean," said Joseph.

How could he put this? Ruben wished that he had been given the skilled tongue of a scribe. But eloquence was certainly not among his gifts. He had wanted to gently lead the discussion to the doubts the other could have about Miriam, but no conversational path had appeared natural to him.

Finally, he blurted out, "She has cheated on you. She is pregnant." Ruben could see that Joseph was very upset with this and regretted having to tell him. Another man might have thought that his wife might have been mistaken. The poor fool could not even imagine such a thing.

"This cannot be," Joseph said slowly.

"Half the women in town know of it," Ruben told him, exaggerating slightly. "You must do something."

"How do they know?"

"Women have ways of knowing things. You are not married, so you have no idea."

"I will have to pray about this," said Joseph.

"Do you know that she is going to Judea?" Ruben was not sure about what this silent man already knew. Perhaps there was a plan to separate by means of the story of the pregnancy of the cousin of the girl.

"Yes, her relative needs her help. She leaves in a matter of days."

"Did they send for her?" Ruben thought he had perceived something furtive in the response of Joseph.

"No, or rather, I don't know. She just knows it, apparently. The cousin is a woman married to a priest and has never before conceived. Miriam says that Elizabeth—that is the woman's name—needs attention. I presume that means she is expecting a child, but I am not sure."

"She *just knows it*? You mean the little girl practices divination?"

"No, but she is a special girl. She is not like others. I believe that she knows something that we have not been able to understand as yet."

"Joseph, this is worse than anything you have said until now," said Ruben.

Necans, who was invisibly present, was repeating the word "witch" to insinuate it into the conversation. "The girl is a witch, witch, witch," the devil communicated to Ruben's unconscious. Humans often fall for that sort of thing.

"I do not understand, Ruben," said Joseph.

Agent Necans realized that the man had a heart that was really pure. It frightened the devil for a moment, and then he continued to repeat the message, "witch," to Ruben.

"Why, she is a witch!" Ruben was surprised to hear himself saying it. "Can't you see what you are falling into? This is much worse than what the women were thinking."

"Ruben, you are worrying about the gossip of women. I have already told you that I will meditate about what I must do."

When Ruben reported the conversation to his wife, she was more alarmed than ever. The strangeness of the case made intervention more necessary. What fools men could be! Rachel let Ruben know that Esther would make a good mate for Joseph. She had not shared this before, but she thought that it would make Ruben feel that he was doing a good deed for Joseph, even though his intended wife, a mere girl, might be stoned.

Although it was unlikely Esther could give him children, she would be loyal to him. This other woman, this young girl, would give him a child that was not his. Joseph and Esther would run the business together, live a good life, and have security. Esther was what Joseph needed. Ruben must communicate that to him. It was for his own good, the poor fool.

During the discussion with his wife, behind closed doors because of the relentless sweeping of the servant girl, Esther arrived. After about an hour with the two women, Ruben was quite anxious to see Joseph again. If he did not do something, Rachel and Esther might cause problems at the synagogue. They would get all the women in a bother and then get all the men upset. Besides, he was convinced something bad was happening. Three devils shadowed him as he walked, proposing all sorts of disasters: Ruben would not be leader of the synagogue because the scandal would out; to avoid this, Joseph should denounce the girl and they would have to stone her; his wife would never forgive him if he allowed things to go any further. He set out immediately to find the poor man.

Of course, Joseph was not alone when Ruben called. The angels from the other side had seen to that. Joachim was with his prospective son-in-law and greeted Ruben enthusiastically. Some of the men in the village had wanted Joachim to be in charge of the synagogue, but he had refused. Nevertheless, Ruben considered him a rival of sorts—having someone around who can do things better than they can is really something quite venomous for the earthlings. But Joachim was so gracious to Ruben that he could not even speak against him about anything. "Until now," whispered Necans to Ruben's unconscious. "*Until now*. All will know that the 'great' person who came from Jerusalem had a scandal in his own house."

These thoughts, insinuated in the idiot's unconscious, made Ruben smile. Even those who like to think of themselves as good cannot help wanting to revenge themselves of slights by others. Human jealousy is one of their most winning attributes and is found in every corner of their existence, even among the "holy" ones.

"You have broken away from your studies of the Holy Scripture, to come to see us," Joachim said to Ruben.

"Yes, I have something pending to talk about with Joseph."

"Well, go right ahead. He is my son-in-law, you know."

According to the local customs, there was nothing that a son-in-law would keep from his father-in-law. Ruben did not have the courage to broach the subject he was dying to talk about in front of the girl's father.

"Yes, it is about a cabinet I would like to order."

"What sort of cabinet?" asked Joachim. Ruben had forgotten that Joachim also had tried his hand at carpentry. He could no longer work that trade, because the old man did not have the physical strength to do so, but he could talk about the design, because he had made such things. "Is this for the synagogue or for your home?"

"Yes," said Ruben.

"Yes which?" asked Joachim. Ruben noticed that Joseph had looked at him directly when he had said yes. There was something wrong with his answer, no doubt, but the blithering idiot could not figure out what it was.

"I'm sorry, but I don't understand your question, Joachim. What do you mean by 'Yes, which?' I came to talk about a cabinet."

Joachim smiled at him, and then said, "Yes, my dear Ruben, but I asked you whether it was for your personal use or for the synagogue."

"Exactly," said Ruben, now blushing.

"Exactly what?" asked Joachim. Ruben was upset that the old man was insisting so much about this fictitious cabinet. The synagogue leader felt that he would be considered a liar because of the stupid thing.

"Perhaps I did not speak well," said Ruben. "Joseph, come with me to the synagogue and I will show you."

"What will you show him?" asked Joachim again. Ruben felt that the old man was persecuting him. Was it just his usual kibitzing or was he meddling to prevent Ruben from telling Joseph the truth? This last thought made Ruben angry. He had been disposed to feel sorry for Joachim in this mess. After all, a man did not always control his daughter. But now Ruben was sure that there was a conspiracy and Joachim knew very well what was going on.

"Joseph, can you come with me this minute?" Ruben asked abruptly. He noticed the two other men exchange a look.

"Of course, Ruben," said Joseph, and he set down the tools that he still had in his hands.

"But you have not answered me yet, about the work. What kind of a cabinet do you want?" Joachim had spoken again, but Ruben was appalled by the old man's aggressiveness and did not even want to answer him. "We will speak later on this topic," Ruben said suddenly with a pained air of false politeness. "I am afraid I must go. Rachel wants to give some ideas, too."

"So it is for the house," said Joachim. "If you are only going to your house, I can come along. I did not want to walk all the way to the synagogue."

"No, we are not going to my house, but to the synagogue."

"But you said your wife..." began Joachim.

Ruben thought, "This terrible old man wants to humiliate me. What an awful person! He said to him, "Father, we will discuss this later," in a voice so forced and artificial that even Joachim was offended by it. Ruben then stepped into the street and said, "Now, Joseph, please."

Of course, Joseph followed the other to the synagogue, which was empty.

"Joseph, you must think of what is happening," said Ruben.

Ruben knew what he should counsel. Joseph should denounce the young sinner and they would have to stone her. Ruben never relished that sort of thing, but there were always men who did. In fact, some women could be counted upon to witness the event. For some of them, a stoning was a kind of entertainment. There was no doubt, however, that the execution of adulterers had a positive social impact, as the devils assigned to Ruben that day insinuated cleverly. People took the Torah more seriously in the wake of such a dramatic example, and that was good. It kept others from adultery. [Devilish logic, indeed. –Informant]

"If...even if this would be true, I would never shed blood," said Joseph. "I would not denounce her."

Ruben thought about this for a moment. Did this mean that Joseph would marry the woman anyway? Would he be like Osee the prophet? This would be a problem not only for Joseph but also for Ruben. His wife would never accept that solution. She and Esther would eventually turn the whole town against Joseph and his bride. Just thinking about the possibility of this pious man married to an unfaithful wife made Ruben shudder.

"What do you propose to do?" asked Ruben somewhat despondently.

"I could divorce her quietly," said Joseph. "She can do what she likes."

The devils monitoring this exchange were appalled by what they heard. Immediately Necans was called into the presence of HSM.

"So how do you feel the plot against the girl is going?" asked HSM.

"It is proceeding very well. What we have achieved thus far is to convince her intended spouse to abandon her."

"Why is the idiot leader of the synagogue letting him forgo the stoning?"

"He is perhaps a weak man who does not want to follow the law to all its consequences," said Necans.

"Shameful. But this monk, Joseph, does not want to stone her?" said HSM (in a tone described as sulky but which I deny because it is very clear that our Commander in Chief was quite correct about the situation. Not stoning the girl meant disaster. As always, our leader was right.)

"That hardly matters. She will be a woman alone in a society that does not appreciate such novelties. Joseph apparently thinks that there is another man to take care of her. We know that such is not the case. She will be alone, with her elderly parents. It is likely that she will be attacked by some members of the community even if Joseph does not consent. That would have been the easiest way to go, but we are talking about a very difficult character. It would be very difficult for someone from his background and personality to have the vindictiveness to lead her execution. But there are others waiting in the wings. The divorce is something we can use."

This mollified Satan, but did not quiet the concerns of Esther, who was told of the latest conversation between Ruben and Joseph.

"Can he be allowed to be indifferent to adultery?" she asked Rachel and Ruben. She was at their home because she had not been able to wait for the news the next day. Necans had put the thought into Esther's head.

"He is the only one who can accuse, of course," Ruben was a little taken back by the fierceness with which Esther spoke.

"We know that he has been tricked. All we have to do is bring out the accusation."

"What proof do we have, Esther? If the husband says nothing, nothing can be done." Ruben was beginning to understand why some people had said that Esther's husband had chosen the better part in dying young.

When Esther was gone, Rachel had some words with

her husband.

"You have not been able to do all we had hoped for," she said. She was playing her husband's conscience like a lute. Humans are not as good as we are in twisting up consciences, but some do a fair job.

"I talked to him, convinced him of the truth of the pregnancy, and he has decided on divorce." Ruben looked at his hands closely as he said this, examining them for some hint of what he could say. He then transferred them to his beard and began twirling hair in his fingers.

"But why wouldn't you have insisted on the marriage question with Esther?"

"I thought the problem was the pregnant girl," Ruben said sheepishly. "I think the other match can be arranged afterwards. The man, after all, is close to his in-laws. He respects them."

"Men never know how to do a thing right when they do something," murmured Rachel.

CHAPTER ELEVEN:
ANOTHER DEAD END

Once again, Ruben went to Joseph's workshop. He immediately felt that it had been a mistake to visit the man again. Of course, he had no choice, however, because his wife would never rest about the affair. He was silent for a time, trying to think of how to begin.

"Well, Joseph," Ruben had had to say finally, "What is new?"

"I have not had much time this week. Many different jobs, including some couches for a Greek merchant in Seforis," the carpenter said somewhat diffidently. "They are for the palace in Tiberias."

This Joseph seemed able to make Ruben feel ill at ease without working too hard at it. Of course, the man Ruben was an idiot. But an idiot with some inkling of the fact of their idiocy, which is a kind of torture for them.

"Some things do not merit delay," Ruben told him with the inimitable tone of authority human beings with very little authority tend to assume.

"Do you mean the couches? I thought you were not keen on our little Herod."

"No," said Ruben, "I mean, well, you know what I

mean. Your decision. About the girl. The divorce. When." He blurted this out because humans are not always able to communicate thoughts well when their endocrinal element in their bloodstream is high. His nervousness was also somaticized and he was very red in the face. Another drawback of the matter/spirit composition is that reactions are filtered through bodies. This is often funny, for us, but it is often awkward for them. It means sometimes that liars are caught by biological reactions outside of their control.

The carpenter took his time. "I plan to say something to them this week. Before she goes down to Ein Karem."

"You must say something today or I shall take it upon myself," said Ruben. He was surprised himself, but that was because Necans had prompted him and the fool did not realize it.

"No, you must not," responded Joseph, with a kind of authority of his own. He obviously scared Ruben with the fierceness of his reply. We, of course, knew that Ruben was a coward, but his reaction was worse than what we might have expected.

"Well, it better be soon," said Ruben, and coughed.

That is another one of those somatizations that the half-clods suffer from. They cough when they are nervous sometimes. But the whole thing spoke of failure. In fact, this was part of the commentary of the High Command on this. There was almost an instant meeting called to evaluate the strategy.

"Necans," said HSM, "We are still awaiting the success of your special mission."

"I think I need some reserves," said Necans. "I need devils to haunt Joseph every step of the way. He is what humans call compassionate. That makes him hesitate to confront the girl. He fears that there will be a scene. What is remarkable about him is a complete absence of anger."

"We will be able to do something about that. Use Belphegor, use Mara."

"I could use more ordinary devils. All they need to do is to remind him at every conscious thought that he is neglecting his duty. He has given his word to the synagogue leader; he has made his decision, etc. His own self-pride will help carry him over the hurdle."

The devils shadowed the carpenter as he walked over to the house of Miriam's parents. They kept up a busy chatter about how scandalous the situation was, until one of them, Chamosh, then thought of another tactic. This has been highlighted in several of the studies made on the failure of the containment plan, because it was a creative sort of strategy.

"Let us make him think he is doing something noble divorcing the girl," he said.

The strategy was agreed upon immediately. They began a constant barrage of thoughts: *Lucky for her that you are a person noble, without any desire of vengeance. She must be in love with some younger man. No doubt he is poorer than you are. They will both be very grateful to you. There is one thing that you can do for them, to set them free. You will have saved a life. She had no right to do this to you, of course.* **And her parents how they presented her to you***! They would force their daughter into a loveless match. All that talk about dedication to God. But there is one thing to do. Let her go into the world.*

This tactic was based on a very good strategy. Without Joseph, the invasion would have had much tougher going.

He was listening to these thoughts pretty well, the devils concluded. The carpenter's intention to leave the girl was still quite on the surface of his mind.

However, there was another obstacle to our plans. When Joseph arrived at the miserable house where Miriam was hiding from us all those years, Joachim stood up to meet him.

"Joseph, I must ask you a favor," he said.

"Of course, Father, whatever you need." This Joseph said, although the devils thought that he really didn't want to do so. In recent studies, this has been questioned, because there is a level of spirit, even in these half-clods, where we cannot go. It was a logical assumption, however. Why would he sacrifice his will to that of someone older, weaker and poorer? What was the hold Joachim had over him? In fact, there was no hold but the carpenter's conscience. Human beings can be so frustratingly inconsistent at times.

"I am afraid to send Miriam to Judea by herself," said Joachim.

"I understand," said Joseph. Meanwhile, the devils tried to make him think that perhaps Joachim was going to tell him about the other man.

"It has not been a week since she mentioned the idea and she is most anxious to go. It is most unlike her not to want to listen to us. She is sure that she must go to our cousin Elizabeth. I never have seen her surer about anything, and I cannot doubt her word. There has never been a moment when she did something capriciously."

The devils were transmitting to the carpenter's consciousness: *Until now! Until now! This is more than a caprice; this is an injustice. What are they trying to cover up? Maybe they are sending her away with the man.*

"What would you like me to do for you?" Joseph said, with a sickeningly self-sacrificing resolution. It really upset the devils around him. Humans who are ready to sacrifice their own wants and needs for others are the bane of our existence. It is to be appreciated that there are so few of them. A day would come when such conduct will be regarded as illness among the humans, a lack of self-esteem. The drumbeat we have kept up for the last century has been to make humans think that self-love is the height of mental health.

"We cannot go ourselves, but she must go." Joachim hesitated. Of course, the devils on duty knew where he was going with this. They started insinuating to Joseph that Joachim wanted to tell him about Miriam's "problem." *Here it comes. They want to get out of here. They will ask you for money. You will pay the price of their sin.*

"We would like to go with her, but we cannot. Could you go?"

"And who would take care of you here?" asked Joseph. The devils were almost too astonished by the question to react. Then they began in earnest. *You have to deliver the girl? The other man was a traveler—somebody passing through! They don't know what to do with her. They think you will forget about this, miscalculate, ignore. This is beyond all bounds. They cannot impose this!*

"We will be all right. There is always a way to stretch the food. Our olive tree has abundant fruit this year. The goat just delivered." The pathetic nature of this response is typical of human affairs. It is hard to explain the lack of logic humans exhibit when they want to believe something. Their existence, which involves consuming enough matter to keep that component of their being functioning, becomes a fantasy of olives and goat cheese.

"I suppose I could leave you some money, once I finish this couch for Cusa," said Joseph. *Idiot! Idiot!* screamed the devils. *They will all laugh at you. Cuckold before marriage! You have no obligation to these people. You have helped them enough.*

"I must pray about this," he said. "If I discern that God wants me to take her to Judea, I will do so. Give me a day to pray about it."

You could go. And leave her there, said a devil. *You could deliver her wherever you like. She has no claims on you! She has betrayed you!*

"Joseph, you have been sent to us by God," said Joachim, quite moved in that strange way of those creatures. These clod-spirits have something called emotions, which run through their bodies and then have an effect on their souls. There is no experience in angelic life to compare with it. We are completely rational, after all, and are not subject to such waves of energy. Because the clodders are material, some have compared the emotions to the pull of gravity that produces the tides and the storms that whirl up in the atmosphere of the earth. Except that these pulls and storms are interior in the case of emotions. Many times, we have occasion to profit by these "natural" forces. Other times they have been our undoing because they can be attached or oriented to selfless ideals and generous impulses, often to the detriment of the person subject to them.

The emotion generated in Joachim stopped Joseph from saying what he wanted to say. That was: "I will go with her to Judah and divorce her quietly." But one clodder often communicates these emotions to another, often it seems without formal communication, although there are eye movements and facial muscle tendencies that they perceive in each other unconsciously. But this wave or energy of emotion took its toll on Joseph. A thought came to his head. "The old man doesn't know." Then another thought, "Would the mother know?"

It was a disastrous scenario. He was analyzing the situation putting the best construction on everyone's behavior. There was something he could do; he would plan something. The devils heard him speak to himself. He would leave money for the old people. They would have the resources to return to Judah after he had divorced the girl. Or they could stay here and the girl would return. He did not have to return to Nazareth. He himself could disappear. He would be the one who abandoned his wife. There were other towns where carpenters could work. He was one man, after all. He would make sure that the girl had a writ of divorce. She must love another! Perhaps that other would meet them. Was that the reason behind the sudden interest in Ein Karem? It would be her way out of Nazareth. That would save her from all problems and Joseph could forget her in peace. But who was the man? He could not figure out who the father of the child could be.

Despite all this nobility of thought, it was evident that the man was perplexed. This was not like Miriam! How would she do something against her parents' will? Joseph's steps back to his workshop were slow. He had decided to buy some food at a stand in the market and not eat at his future in-laws. The devils watched him and waited. There had to be some weakness in all this. There had to be a way to get him to expose the girl.

The devils hurried Ruben to the workshop. He had to be spurred on because he was weak, but also lazy, and laziness is ironically and very occasionally a terrible obstacle for evil in humans. At last, they prevailed upon him to walk to where Joseph was sitting in silence, sharpening some of his tools. He had run out of things to say to Joseph. He knew that if he went to the workshop, he would have to report to Rachel everything the two had said. And she would be disappointed if the marriage to Esther were not the center of the conversation with Joseph.

"Well, have you come to some kind of conclusion, Joseph?" asked Ruben.

"I have," said Joseph in a quiet tone.

"And may I ask what it is that you will do?" asked Ruben expectantly. This had to be good news. The only decision, thought the synagogue leader, would be to eliminate the adulteress.

"You will know tomorrow," said Joseph and looked at Ruben straight in the eyes. The latter was quite uncomfortable about this. He looked down at his feet. He also asked himself why he always had to suffer the consequences of Rachel's tendency to get too involved in other people's lives.

"That's all you are going to say?" asked Ruben after Joseph had proceeded to plane a great piece of tree trunk.

"That is all I am going to say," said Joseph stolidly.

Naturally, we were confronted with mystery, which we hate. The propensity of the enemy to keep us guessing is perhaps what most annoys us. Joseph acted as if he didn't know that Ruben was crazed with curiosity. He kept silence. Stolidity is the opposite of what we want. Instability, capriciousness, volatility are the human qualities that serve us best in our struggle. In tranquility we find a wall that prevents us from allowing the humans to do what they do worst, contradict themselves *a outrance* [Apparently the devil likes to quote phrases in French, too. –Informant] They can be their own worst enemies.

This Joseph was one of those disgusting creatures who did not have the courage of human incoherence. They are supposed to fall, to act on impulse, they *should* mess things up, and their capacity to act contrary to their principles is their (and our) greatest asset. The cautious prudence with which Joseph deliberated and prayed and waited are among the more shameful aspects of this painful episode in the history of our war for real justice.

"As I suspected," said Ruben, a bit hurt. He used a tone that humans have recourse to when they want to sound ironic, but irony was not Ruben's strong suit, let us say. Necans, who was there, could not help but be amused, although he was also puzzled.

CHAPTER TWELVE:
PULCHERIA

[Different writer? Several new words are used that were not elsewhere in the dossier. -ed.]

His Satanic Majesty lost patience with Necans' plan. Although it was not yet evident to all (read that: Necans and company) that it would not succeed, nevertheless, the peerless perspicacity of our great leader no doubt showed him that another strategy was in order. HSM called Moloch to him and assigned him the case.

Moloch immediately had a plan. He went that night to a certain Syro-Phoenician woman who lived in Seforis. She was an expert in many things female. Pulcheria (by that point a devilishly ironic name because she was not at all beautiful even in the manner of the half-clods). Her life had been dedicated, you might say, to the god Eros, who takes more revenge on human beings than can ever be calculated. The wrinkles of her skin, the fatigue that had nested permanently in her bones, and the yellowish color that passed from her skin to the whites of her eyes, all of that was nothing compared to what had happened to her soul.

Pulcheria was believed to have the power to give a woman a potion to make a man fall in or out of love with her. She could also, according to the same ignorant, superstitious crowd, help a woman—even an older one—conceive, by the magic of herbs and the light of the new moon. She could also help women who might have "a problem" if they conceived, especially when their husbands were away or before a man had claimed them as a spouse. That is how Moloch had come to know her. When infant sacrifice was abolished in Palestine, he had specialized in "taking care of inconveniences."

The old hag was about to fall asleep when the knock came on her door.

"Who is it?" she asked nervously.

"Someone who needs your help," said a voice that made even this hardened woman a little afraid. There was a sweetness to the voice that sounded completely artificial, something inherently contradictory, like an iron fist hiding in a velvet glove, but with a tear in the glove revealing the metal.

Through a crack in the door, Pulcheria saw that the man wore a Roman uniform. That was strange because this was Herod's kingdom. She heard a horse behind him breathing heavily, though, and presumed he was some kind of messenger. Perhaps he was lonely that night. But could he be lonely enough to be interested in a dried-up old bag of bitterness like her?

"This is not a time for respectable visitors," she said in Greek.

"Perhaps not, but I am in need of your services," said the voice again, which gave her goose bumps. This is something that happens to the skin of half-clods when there is sufficient cold outside or fear within. [There is a diabolic footnote to this: "Goose bumps are interesting, because they have such a dual function." –Informant] There was such malevolence in the tone and the confidence of the interlocutor, the old woman was afraid.

She opened the door a crack. "I don't want to wake my husband," she said.

"You have no husband, you miserable old woman," said the Roman soldier, but in an odious tone not even military men were capable of.

"What is it you need?" asked the woman.

"There is a certain young girl. She has a problem."

"What sort of problem?"

"One you are used to dealing with, witch," again the voice was gravelly and aggressive, much different from the sweet tones it used at first.

"I do not know what you mean," the old woman said fiercely.

"You know precisely what I mean, you old snake. Let me in for a moment and I will explain what you must do tomorrow."

Pulcheria opened the door without another word. What would this man do to her? She had no idea, but she could not help but obey him.

The next morning, ill-humored more even than was normal for this embittered woman, she went to seek Esther. They had had only a nodding acquaintance before this. Even that was putting things very generously. Someone like Esther could never even say hello to the old hag. Pulcheria half expected to find the Roman soldier at the inn. She could not help thinking about him and how odd it was that he was travelling alone. A man of his rank would have to be accompanied by some soldiers. How had he found his way to her little house and how did he know what she did?

"Last night a man came to my house," she told Esther all at once, and then regretted her starting that way because of the look on the other woman's face.

"He was a Roman soldier; I think a centurion. A very bad man, I think. But he told me to talk to you about a young girl in this village whom he—"

"Did he say her name?" Esther had practically jumped at this news.

Pulcheria had looked directly at the other woman at this point. Her throat was fat, and she had a double chin, with full cheeks. You could see from her face, which did not have wrinkles, that Esther had had an easy life. No doubt she had never known what it was to make do without servants, thought Pulcheria coldly, but now the fat thing was fascinated with the story.

"He feels sorry for the girl," she told the other woman, whose eyes shown with delight.

"He cannot respond for her. She is sick, and he wondered if I could help her. Her parents have finally found her a husband."

"Why would you come to me?" asked Esther, suddenly nervous enough to look around to see if anyone noticed they were talking.

"He said you might know the girl," said the Syro-Phoenician.

"I don't think so," lied Esther, and Pulcheria of course knew she was lying. Nevertheless, it is a remarkable characteristic of these clodlings that they can continue to lie even when their listener knows the truth. There are even some of them who can make people forget the truth and believe the lie. These include some of the real movers and shakers of their history. They are actually rewarded for not telling the truth. "Tell a lie with a straight face," said one of the damnedest of the crew, "and someone is bound to believe it and even defend it." He now is much less cheerful than he was when he made the observation, I assure you.

"If you did, he said that you would point her out to me, and he wanted me to ask her how she was feeling."

"He didn't say her name?"

"Yes, he said it was..." Here the old fool of a woman forgot the name. It took Moloch several minutes of steady suggestion before she remembered. "Oh, yes, it was Miriam."

Esther's eyes opened wide at this. Pulcheria could not miss the interest.

"But why have you come to me? You don't know me."

"No, just the name of him who was your husband."

"How would you know my husband's name?" asked Esther sharply. No doubt she was thinking that her husband had had something to do with the old hag before her. Human beings are quite finite in so many respects, but they have an infinite capacity for jealousy.

"Everyone knows the innkeeper of a small town," said Pulcheria. She was happy to see the discomfort in the other's face. Obviously, Esther wanted to know something more, and did not want to send Pulcheria away, although she was clearly disgusted by her.

"I might know the young girl you speak of," Esther said slowly. "But how can I hope to direct you to her?"

"He said that she would be going to the well near her house in the morning. He suggested that you could tell me which of the young girls was the one I needed to speak with."

"But how could I be seen walking with a...gentile? You know about our laws."

"And how they suit you when you want to abide by them, yes. He suggested you go to the well looking for a servant girl you thought was taking too much time."

"And how does he know how I treat my servants?" asked Esther, a bit afraid.

"He seemed to know many things. Strange I had never seen him before, but he acted as if he was quite familiar with me and with everybody around here."

Esther looked even more worried.

"I will tell you what to do. We will go to the well, you following me by a distance of at least ten meters. [In all the references in the devilish works measures are given in metric. -Informant] I will greet the girl—her name is Miriam—if that is the one you mean. More than that I cannot do."

Esther was already planning what she would say to Rachel. The story of the Roman soldier was irresistible.

At the well, they found Miriam. Esther greeted her solemnly and asked her how her mother Anne was. Then she hurried off to visit Rachel. Pulcheria waited at some distance and talked to Miriam when the latter was drawing water. The girl had been the last of the long line of women at the well.

"I have been told you are not feeling well," said Pulcheria in a whisper.

"I am well, thank you," said the girl.

Obviously, she was one of those who had been trained not to talk to strangers, but was too kind not to respond to the conversation even of an old stranger.

"A man talked to me about you. A very strange man who appeared at my door in the night. He appeared to know many things. I am not sure he was even a man. There was something about him, something strange. It made me a little afraid."

This seemed to interest the girl a great deal. Moloch was, of course, prompting the wicked old woman to say what she did so that the girl would think of an angel, like the one who had visited her.

"What, what did he say about me?" asked the girl. She looked so intently into Pulcheria's eyes that the latter shrank back a bit. It was a little frightening to see such innocence when she had expected something else.

"He said that you were 'sick' and that maybe I could help you," said Pulcheria again in a whisper.

The girl closed her eyes a moment. Was she going to cry? The old hag had no idea what she was dealing with. Moloch's idea was not a bad one, but to rely on an old witch to broach the subject of the potion was idiotic. Because that is what the wrinkled bag of bones next did. She could prepare a soup, she said, something that would make Miriam feel better. She had helped other girls in the same way.

Pulcheria had said this last looking down at the ground, hoping that she was doing this in the humblest way possible. The centurion had promised her even more than the purse she had buried in her house if she was successful in this. But when she raised her eyes to the young girl's, she saw a kind of bright coldness that pierced her to the heart.

"I am not sick," said the girl. "He must have been mistaken. Perhaps he was talking about another girl."

"I don't think so."

Tell her that she will be better off. Tell her that she could be stoned to death. She was in a perilous condition. A simple potion and her life would be better. Joseph was waiting for her in marriage. Could she believe in anything so strange as what had happened to her? She would feel much better if she let Pulcheria help her. She should think about raising a child—if they let her live—all alone. Did she want to see her child die before her? Would she be willing to do what she would have to do to survive? We will get her a better husband besides, one who has money.

Moloch was making the old woman's head spin with ideas. She repeated them, slowly, but not all that coherently. She was there to help. Miriam must think that she was on her own. Her parents would not understand. Joseph could not possibly accept what was going on. She would feel better. One bitter draught and she would be released of her worry.

The young virgin supposedly blushed; her cheeks were flushed by emotion. (Yes, even she!) That redness was to have unfortunate consequences for us, as Moloch was to find out. The old hag Pulcheria, seeing the emotion on the young earthling's visage, herself was moved a bit. This led her to feel what humans call embarrassment, which is an inconvenient emotion of contradiction. Supposedly they feel that they are committing some sin, or something that will be criticized, and that is somaticized in a general feeling of personal disarray and a certain warmth and redness in the face, usually caused by the dilation of capillary beds. It is all part of the inefficiency of their intellectual powers, according to some scholars. What they cannot do by means of their poor intellect, they sometimes supply by what is called instinct. It is a pre-conceptual reaction that we do not experience.

"I must go," the girl said, tears in her eyes. But they were not tears of indecision. She had not for a moment wanted to listen to Pulcheria. Her tears were for the ugliness of what the old hag was proposing. This sent the old witch into a dither. Not only would there not be another bag of coins for her, but she was also suddenly aware of her own dirtiness. How could she have made a life of doing such things? She was ashamed of herself, as odd as that sounded to her who had known no shame for so many years.

Something else happened that Moloch only confided to His Supreme Majesty. He tried to get a look at the girl's soul while the old woman was looking at her. The intensity of pain it caused him had more than surprised him. He could not bear to look at the light in the girl's soul. Other people had refused his suggestions, even among the poor who had resisted sacrificing their children to him against all custom in their villages. But this girl had scared him. His Supreme Majesty had mocked him for his confession, as the transcripts show.

"You could not look at the little girl? You who have done so much and will do even more as time goes by? Get out of my presence instantly. Vermin! Disgusting coward! A little girl shall frighten you? I will show you what it means to be scared..." [The transcript goes on for some time with insults, for which there is an endless creativity in hell. -Informant]

CHAPTER THIRTEEN:
PULCHERIA ESCAPES US

As the girl walked to her home, with the heavy water jar on her head, the old woman moved on, feeling a greater weight on her shoulders. Her heart pounded with anxiety. Pulcheria returned to her miserable hovel, her soul darkened by yet more sins. The walk to Seforis took more than an hour, however. The pounding of her heart had eased up, and she began thinking of how to console herself. She remembered that she had not counted the gold coins in the cloth bag the Roman soldier had given her. How much money could it be? They looked like gold coins. If so, she would have enough money to leave this town and go to the coast. She could set herself up in Sidon; perhaps start her own business, with any number of girls working for her. Already she began to see herself as a rich matron, bedecked with jewels and drinking from silver wine cups.

These last thoughts had given a spring to her wretched steps. She was winded by the time she got to the house, but determined to spend some time passing the coins from one hand to another. Even if they were not gold, even if they were only copper, there was more money in the bag than she had seen in a long time.

She closed the door carefully and bolted it with the crooked piece of wood. The devil on guard was waiting with glee and watched her every movement. Although she was not aware of the surveillance, her natural precaution with money made her look around the house to guarantee that no one was seeing her. She moved a carpet and then dipped both hands in the sandy soil that covered the wood lid of a box interred under the floor. The devil noted with satisfaction that her posture resembled that of those who pray—on her knees, head bowed, with an intensity of attention revealed on her face.

At first she didn't sense the smell, apparently. Then its persistence made her look around impatiently. What was it? The devil who was lucky enough to be present would recount this to many. Had an animal died? Had someone broken into the house? Was this a revenge for something she had done? The smell got fiercer and fiercer.

When she finally dug the box out of the ground, opened it and took the bag out, she had her veil over her nose and mouth. The odor of corruption was so strong that she could barely breathe. When she opened the bag the smell of decay was so overpowering, she fell backwards. It was a stupid joke on the part of Moloch, making her think she had some coins when it was really a bag of offal. We paid for the mistake, as will be seen.

Perhaps Moloch really did think his *petit jeu d'esprit* was going to be enough to finish off the wretched ruin of a woman. That was his testimony at the inquest. What is certain is that the woman ran out of the house. They say that sometimes humans have an uncanny perception of our presence. Maybe she knew that Moloch was there trying to get a good laugh at her expense. Anyway, it backfired.

The woman became ashamed of what she did. This is a troublesome custom of humans. They collaborate freely in something wrong, making themselves rebels as much as we are, well not as much, but as much as they are capable. Then they repent. Although shame has its uses, especially when it is based on human respect and can inhibit much goodness, sometimes it works the other way. The dirty decrepit old wench was sorry for what she had suggested to the one who was the mother of *Him Whom We Would Rather Not Name*.

She ran out into the sunshine, still smelling the awful odors of hell that Moloch had captured in the little bag. In her haste it is surprising that she was able to think so well, but somehow she managed to return to Nazareth in less than an hour's time. In that pitiful town, she was somehow able to find Miriam's house immediately. Some authors have claimed that Pulcheria had the help of her Custodian (as we call those angels who submit to the tyranny of the Three-in-One and "watch over" half-clods) who intervened and let her intercept the path of the young Miriam very close to the door of her parents' home. It is noteworthy that although we underestimate at times their interventions because they seem less energetic and creative than ours, Guardian Angels can really upset our plans.

"Forgive me," begged the disloyal woman, complete with that human trick of tears.

"God bless you, old woman," said the young girl in a voice that sounded to the hag as the choirs of the Seraphim, those disgusting obsequious and servile singers of the celestial courts (of course, I do not mean any of our comrades, who, besides, have lost the power to sing).

"Thank you, my child. I am sure that God is with you, may He keep you in His care," said Pulcheria.

That was not the only outrage. One moment she is involved in trying to tear from his mother's womb the great Terrorist of History and then the ugly hag is giving out blessings. Worse was to come. As she walked slowly home, she was in a daze. This led Moloch and her anti-Custodian to slack off.

Her brittle old heart was about to break and Moloch did not pay attention. He was already thinking about how to encounter Joseph and move to another plan. The devil assigned to Pulcheria apparently did not notice the shortness of breath, the slowing step, the limited vision. No doubt he was thinking of other assignments, more interesting than an old woman whose time even for sinning was running short.

Pulcheria did not reach her miserable dwelling. She stopped outside a palatial home in Seforis where there was a Greek theater. There were all sorts of people there for an entertainment. They were laughing in the theater, at some play by Menander. She stopped in the street outside the great house. There were Roman soldiers there, no doubt to guard some guest at the house. She wondered if the centurion who had visited her was in the audience. At first the guards did not even notice her. She just stood there for a moment and then collapsed to the earth.

Moloch said that he heard the terrible music of the angels taking her soul to safekeeping and was astonished. We had not only lost the battle of Miriam and the baby, but we also couldn't even manage pathetic Pulcheria. Moloch had to appear before the inquest, but his *aide de camp*, the assistant devil assigned to Pulcheria, bore the brunt of the criticism and sentencing. He had been derelict in duty. He had presumed what he should never have presumed.

"Her soul was a mess," he had whined at the court martial, "Who could have thought the brief encounter with the girl would turn things around?"

As we have already pointed out, it was not just the brief encounter that had caused the loss of Pulcheria. Moloch had overplayed his hand with the stench of hell. Although he argued that he had understood that the fragility of the woman's health had made it logical that she would die from the shock of discovering his joke, no one believed him.

"I tell you, it was the girl. When I tried to look at her, I was practically blinded. She must represent some kind of secret weapon. We need better technology to respond to it." [The word translated here as "technology" is one for which I doubt there is a human equivalent. How could angels use tools or develop techniques? However, it seems to be about something learned and useful. I could not find another word. –Informant]

At that point the court officials and the audience of the usual hangers-on broke into derisive laughter. Moloch, who had been important enough to have his own shrines and ritual, was punished for nearly two thousand years. Only lately has HSM generously conceded to him a rehabilitation and restoration to the rank of arch-demon.

The punishment could not undo the damage done, however. And the lessons of this skirmish were not understood or were not incorporated in future planning, which will be obvious from what is below.

CHAPTER FOURTEEN:
MATCHI-MANITU

[Evidently by another demonic historian. –Informant]

It was obvious that the plan that had been followed was mistaken. Many believe that the error was trying to do something directly with the young girl. The security around her was so tight that it would have been impossible even for the smartest devil to touch her. It should have been clear that it was only through another human, and then, directly, not through some kind of insinuation, that something could be done. The whole operation with Pulcheria had been flawed. The idea that the young girl with a legion of angels about her could have fallen into the trap of "getting rid of" the child she bore—in the deliciously absurd language of the half-clods—was an equivocation.

She did not sense the presence of the army of angels and it was partially shielded even from our eyes, but it was real. That was why for centuries there has been discussion of "secret weapons" and "stealth shields," etc. Many explain the fact that we had no idea of how many angels were detailed to her by the idea of "vertical guard" as opposed to a "horizontal" one. That unapproachable light, which some have insisted was due to the subject's sinlessness, according to the Vertical Theory, was the intensity of myriads of angels concentrated on the human soul of her child—the infamous "Number 2."

Part of the reason for the misunderstanding was not knowing how low "Number 1" would grovel in order to "save" the human race. It is still quite astonishing the humiliation implied in the joining of the person of "Number 2" with a human soul. What disarmed our Intelligence Service was the extraordinary simplicity of the plan. If you want to save these miserable creatures, you must become one of them. Not only would we *not* want to save them, but we would also certainly *not* want to become one of them. Nevertheless, the *Awful Three in One* decided on the folly. That is still the heart of our struggle with them. We try to make "lost" that which *We All Know Who* wants to "save." Our success depends on our entering the imagination of the pathetic creatures and conducing them to their destruction. Nevertheless, we do not get inside as our enemy gets inside. Nor would we want to do so.

[The above section is a paragraph that was floating around on the "Infernal Net." Its interest for me is that it proves that the devils can "do" Incarnation Theology. I wonder how that Russian Dostoyevsky knew to make the Anti-Christ a theologian in his book. How did he get that insight without all the trouble I had to suffer to get close to these monsters? –Informant]

Pulcheria dead, Moloch out of the way, another devil had to take charge. The one selected by HSM was one called Matchi-Manitu, who later was given charge of some North American indigenous people. The name means

"Spirit of the Moon" and that was fitting because this devil was an expert in working on humans in their sleep. The indigenous of North America considered him the cause of tempests on bodies of water. His specialty for a long time was producing tempests within a person.

He was presented with the case of Joseph.

"Of course, we should let him put Miriam away. That will put her in the most vulnerable position possible. But it is important not to take risks with these spirits-chained-to-clay. I will insinuate myself into his dreams this night and ensure that he will put the girl away."

Satan was skeptical. That has been well-documented despite the usual Michaelist revisionism. Some have dared to speculate that HSM was taken in by Matchi-Manitu's strategy. Really, he only allowed it to be put in effect, but only as part of a whole range of activities that were meant to forestall the birth of the Messianic individual. If for a time it appeared that HSM had backed the dream gambit, this was only part of his command of the situation. He obviously knew it would not work out completely, but it could have contributed to a global solution to the problem. Which was, of course, to pretend to fail at stopping the Invasion, setting up a trap. [New concept. –Informant]

"Go ahead. It appears that this Joseph is a dreamer like his namesake."

Some very bold angels have dared conclude from that single sentence that Satan was pinning his hopes on convincing Joseph by means of a dream. Objectively, all that the remark means is that the subject could be influenced by stimulated unconscious activity, i.e. dreams. Michaelist factions are constantly trying to make a case for the fallibility of HSM. They will never succeed because there is no other authority beneath the world like that of Lucifer. All devils are subject to his will, even those who would rather not be under his dominion. This will all be brought out in the open when the final battle for the world begins. Meanwhile we go on defeating the enemy one soul at a time.

So Matchi-Manitu waited till evening the day of the death of Pulcheria and went to work. Joseph tarried a bit longer on his prayers than was usual. That was, of course, a very inauspicious development. "If humans would spend more time on their evening prayers, we would have much more trouble than we have." This is something that is in the most basic texts of study in the War College. Joseph was in an exceptionally concentrated state of prayer for quite a while that night. For one part of it he left his humble house/ carpentry shop and was looking up at the stars in what the devils close by considered "a forlorn emotional state." Pure speculation. Because he was in very deep prayer, there was no way of knowing even his emotional state. The invisibility produced by contemplation in the human soul does not permit our seeing into it, of course.

Finally, the prayer was over and Matchi-Manitu could get started. He wove a dream for Joseph based on his Essene past. As the dreamer looked around, he saw the desert all around, complete with the roaring of lions in the distance, something that had always attracted Joseph's attention, perhaps because he very superficially associated the wild beasts with his having descended from one who was called the "Lion of Judah."

Then it was suddenly day (apparently humans can dream of extended time periods in the few minutes a dream takes). The compression of experience is interesting to us who never sleep and thus never dream, of course, but it is another example that although they are often so pitiful in questions of logic, the humans are symbolizing creatures. With a few sensory cues, they can somehow go beyond the place where they find themselves. Really, humans are caught in a very specific reality but are always imagining other alternatives. Their mobility is risible, and time and distance are felt by them as hindrances, no doubt because they are only "part" spiritual.

That explains why in a dream the sense of time is very elastic and a few minutes can be felt to be years and the action that takes place shifts from scene to scene as if the poor stunted creatures had our ability to displace their wretched little selves with ease as we do. Another quirk of matter when it mixes with spirit, which is why the better sort of spiritual creatures were always against what we called "the experiment."

"As we cannot dream, we sometimes can underestimate and other times overestimate their value in terms of provocation of conduct." We all remember that from Ursheol's famous text. However, this is what happened that night with Matchi-Manitu. Dreams for humans sometimes are nothing else than a response to the half-awake brain to material stimuli. A man who sleeps under a leaky roof dreams of being on a boat at sea. Other dreams are a type of wish fulfillment. The boy gets the girl, the man wins the lottery, and the woman finds the love of her life. Apparently, the human unconscious is always writing scenarios based on fantasies, memories and responses to stimuli not always conscious. We who have no unconscious are not always able to understand the pathetic little monsters for that reason.

Matchi-Manitu did his work. There have been some who claimed that he did not prepare the dream as he should have. That is not the truth. It was a very subtle kind of operation and he was a very careful player with humans. His basic gambit or strategy was not without some merit. Really, this author considers that his failure was more the result of sabotage by the enemy than any other reason. In short, to use a line of a poet who in the end managed to escape our clutches, he was "more sinned against than sinning."

So, M&M searched the records and found out that Joseph had been close to one of the Essene masters when he had lived in the monastery near the Dead Sea. This was one Isaiah, who had given Joseph formation in his novitiate. Originally from Jerusalem, he was from a Zadokite priestly family and had a tremendous knowledge of the Torah. He was also a man who lived very ascetically. He never ate meat, for instance, and survived on bread and water and a few vegetables. Isaiah had been named for a priest and prophet who was supposedly some kind of ancestor, although our records indicate this claim was false, thanks to a secret adultery promoted by one of our agents assigned to the Temple area. There were, however, High Priests in his genetic history.

In Joseph's dream, Isaiah appeared to Joseph as the latter was engaged in drawing water from the Essene wells. Since they lived on the edge of a desert and took frequent baths for ritual purposes, water-carrying loomed large in the life of the community.

"Set down the water jar," Isaiah ordered in the dream and instantly Joseph obeyed him. The man was docile in life, so why wouldn't he be in his unconscious creative stream?

"Master, is it thou who speakest to me?" Many have criticized the stilted language that M&M used in this dream. They did not know the Essenes. The ascetical life they lead demanded a special language. It was part of the whole ambience of disgusting fidelity to the will of WAKW that characterized the miserable community. Their thoughts were different and so they used a different diction.

"Yes, Joseph, thou art correct," said the virtual marionette in the dream. Sure, it sounded like one of those awful earthling Bible epics, but I think the diction was not unjustifiable.

"Let the girl go," said Isaiah. "She loveth another."

"How do you know?" asked Joseph. This shows a kind of critical spirit that M&M did not expect from a man so famously humble.

"There is a knowledge whereof man knows not the coming hither," said Isaiah. It was lame, but M&M was scrambling, because he feared Joseph might wake up.

"And what shall I do?" asked Joseph.

"You shall come back to us, Joseph. We are your brothers. Your time of probation has ended. We want to see you again."

"But you are dead, Master Isaiah!" That meant that he would be calling Joseph not to the community on the shores of the Dead Sea but to Sheol. This apparent lapse by M&M has been much commented upon. He could not have forgotten that Isaiah was dead. Angels, after all, are not forgetful like humans, who confuse all manner of things. It seems that their agent intellects get clogged up by matter like some of the drains in their ramshackle lodgings. It is a disputed point, and some of our best demonologists disagree on why the silly things can know something and then it slips away from them. What would our life be like if we would forget things? (Obviously, a lot happier, said a wag, who may be still in the deepest pit of hell.) How could you not be happy if you could forget reality? Anyway, it is clear that M&M did not make a mistake, although the persistent literalism of Joseph may give the wrong impression.

"The community is alive and I live in it, as you will live. Let the girl have her life. You have done your penance, and you have expiated your sins; come and be with us as we wait for God's will to be realized."

Matchi-Manitu then evoked the singing of the Essenes, something that had always moved Joseph, as well it might. The Enemy had taught the monks to sing. When the community was wiped out, it took humans several centuries to develop a chant as mystical as that of Qumran. Music is analogous for humans, obviously. What we can appreciate in a purely spiritual way they sense through the medium of their despicable clay. Even the notes which are the elements of their version of music are somehow products of reverberations of applied motion on different pieces of matter. That is why they have those silly pictures of angels with instruments in their hands. As if a spirit could play a wind instrument? With what kind of breath does a spiritual being have to force movement through a stick or a bronze tube? Even their "Holy" Book panders to their small minds with images of angels with trumpets. Pathetic.

Joseph settled back to slumber to the tune of the

chanting of the Essenes. He seemed prepared to follow the course of action that would have been much more favorable for us fighting off the invasion. The girl would end up with the aging parents, Joseph would leave the scene, and the vulnerability of her situation would provide us with more opportunity to stop the whole operation in its infancy, as the foolish little creatures call a period that is really like extra-uterine gestation.

Remember, Joseph had already adverted to his intention to give the girl a divorce. But Matchi-Manitu had forgotten something very important in understanding the enemy; something we can never forget in *Unser Kampf*, and that is that there are no depths to which they will not descend. Of course, I am speaking in plural and we all know about that. When the playing field was level, the victory was ours. Joseph would go back to the desert and we would have "Peace in Our Time," or something similar. The constant aggression of the enemy power, the injustice of the tactics used to reclaim the mongrel being that is half clay and half spirit and the infinite inability to leave well enough alone is what Matchi-Manitu forgot.

The Other Side decided on a direct intervention. Gabriel was given the task, which indicates how that lowlife no-talent has been able to rise in the order of things in the enemy camp. I insert here the famous words of our "professor" about the archenemy Gabriel: "Of course, he would not be so important if some of the most talented had not declared themselves for Independence. The tyranny of the Three-in-One has had to use the second string, as the clodlings say. Gabriel is certainly not a subtle spirit, and his conversations with the humans show either how little he esteems their intelligence or his concern for their understanding even at the risk of losing angelic dignity in discourse. Shameful."

Gabriel's words are found in a garbled form in one of the four essays in biography that have sustained a guerrilla movement against our dominion on earth. I say garbled because they have been edited to such an extent that they are nowhere near an exact account. With telegraphic style, the angel says to purported "father-to-be," "Joseph, son of David, fear not to take unto thee Mary thy wife, for that which is conceived in her is of the Holy Ghost. And she shall bring forth a son: and thou shalt call his name Jesus. For he shall save his people from their sins."

For the record, the dream was much longer than that. It began recalling the genealogy of this same Joseph of Bethlehem....

CHAPTER FIFTEEN:
JOSEPH'S DREAM

It is a peculiar trait of the half-clods that they are very proud about their ancestry. This is hard for us who have been brought to existence "at once and for all time" to understand. The febrile engendering of new humans, instead of making them ashamed of their origins, fills them with pride. They like to recount the names of their ancestors. As if it were some kind of prestige to be the result of so much mingling of matter. (Of course, we have been able to take advantage of some illusory pretensions by helping some humans to dramatize histories of their supposed families. The success of several webpages in this respect has a certain charm. Pride, in whatever form, is always welcome to us.)

The people of Israel, the famous "Chosen People," have been especially remarkable in their memory of their ancestors. Whole dreary pages of the "Book" list name after name of the poor half-clods. The Chosen People, with more honesty than many other groups, include with those names information that many of the personages involved might rather suppress. As an example of this, there are prostitutes and liars in the "family" tree of the Anointed

One, the exalted Number Two. It is part of the human's knack of making virtues of necessities. Instead of hiding the humiliating elements, they show them off at times, a strategic decision that is often overlooked in our daily combats. It is illogical and thus hard for us to take into account. Humility is anathema to us to the same degree that pride is agreeable.

So, this "archangel" Gabriel—I use the quotation marks advisedly—began to present to Joseph in his dream the messianic succession. Remember that time is elastic in dreams, and in seconds, plots can be sketched out which give the pathetic beings the sensation of years of experience. And so Joseph, in his dream, saw Abraham and spoke to him. What the two said to each other has not been preserved verbatim, because the devil in charge of monitoring Joseph thought he had the evening free after the intervention of Matchi-Manitu. Here we see an important detail in our great war of continued independence of the TT. We must be vigilant every second so as not to give up all the ground that we have in our possession—practically the whole planet. The guerrillas will not prevail; we shall retain sovereignty. [The style of this part of the manuscript made the one who recovered it from the pages of infernal Internet think that this was a kind of material for diabolical refresher courses. I find this hard to square with what we know about angelic intelligence, but the ultra-obvious sententiousness does have a kind of infernal tone to it. -ed.]

So, our enemy Gabe trots out Abraham, who looks into the eyes of Joseph and says, "You are the key to His plan." Of course, this makes mush of the said subject's emotions because who of his people did not want to be connected with Abraham, the much-vaunted "father" of the faithful, and also to have a role in what we know now as the Invasion? Joseph would have done anything at that point, but Gabriel cannot be accused of subtlety. He went on through all of Joseph's ancestors, including Judah, who thought he had carnal commerce with a prostitute and then found out it was actually his widowed daughter-in-law, and Rahab, the awful lady of the twilight who saved the Israelite spies in Jericho (another fiasco that played a part in one of the court-martials of the much too ambitious Baal), and then the Moabitess Ruth, whose foreignness did not prevent her from being the great grandmother of a king. These unlikely heroines were followed by Bathsheba, who is not always named, but whose adultery is alluded to implicitly. Last and of course not least for our interests came Miriam, the one who was "espoused" to Joseph. Another case of a woman of peculiar circumstances, in this case her soul's blindingly close union with *You Know Who*.

The dream concluded with the famous words, "Do not fear to take the woman into your custody." The message was clear, the action of the miserable carpenter, a monk manqué, was heroic. And these petty clodlings all want to be heroes, even the most preposterous cases. There are some who say that such a dream was impossible to circumvent or neutralize. I prefer not to speculate about the matter. What the incident does show, however, is how much the enemy wants to take this planet away from us, this polluted, wasteful wonderland of vice that we have had dominion over since the first half-clods were formed of this wretched clay.

The dream, of course, did not stop with Abraham. The Trinitarian Tyranny did not take that chance. Joseph saw all of his ancestors in a kind of parade, like Shakespeare's Banquo. [One of several times that Shakespeare is mentioned by devils. The Informant held that it was because the devils were envious of his imagination and therefore the poet had been an object of their special, but apparently ultimately frustrated, attention. –ed.] Thus he spoke to David, the sinner without valor (every time he did something wrong, he would come crawling back to Number 1, writing poems that are still repeated in the resistance movement) and Zerubbabel (this was overkill, because no one gives a damn about Zerubbabel, despite his mention in the "Book." Even the guerrilla forces generally know *nothing* about him).

Joseph got up before the first light, walked over to his "wife's" parents and managed to get them to let him take Miriam to Elizabeth her kinswoman the next day. Of course, the narrations in the third biography of "Number 2" give the impression that Miriam went down to Ein Karem immediately after the disaster of the start of the Invasion, when two whole weeks had gone by. The parents of the woman decided Joseph's offer was a great blessing. The paupers really had had no means of sending the girl down to Judea, despite Joachim's talk of a caravan. We could have done something with a caravan. Of course, that was where Joseph fit in, as far as the plan goes, because he had just made some money and had the wherewithal to buy the miserable donkey that carried the "glorious" mother of the King down the broken roads and through the desert places in order to get to her cousin's home.

Joseph was a man who did not stop to think about alternative interpretations of his dreams. That is why the two set out the same day and, by a tremendous error of calculation, were not prevented from doing so by our troops.

CHAPTER SIXTEEN:
THE TWO FRIENDS

Nazareth had much to talk about in the following days. Obviously one of the most delicious qualities humans have is their penchant to discuss each other *in absentia*. Rachel and Esther learned that Miriam and Joseph had gone away exactly 24 hours after the fact. A few hours later they were told that Pulcheria had been found dead in Seforis. Ruben was surprised at how shocked Esther was of the news. How had she known about Pulcheria? He was about to ask her when she said, "You have heard of her." He had to think fast in order to say that he had heard she had caused many problems in Seforis. [Infernal asterisks in the text indicate that this was some kind of diabolical joke. – Informant]

Perhaps it was the cleanup operation that distracted our forces from interrupting the journey of the mother of Number 2 (the absurdity of "motherhood" attached to a person with relation to a subject which is spiritual, eternal and infinite is of course shocking to me, as it is to anyone without our sphere of influence, nevertheless—how else to refer to her?).

HSM was, quite logically, deeply disappointed with the

carelessness and stupidity of his underlings, which could not reflect anything shameful or inferior with regard to his person. There was another meeting of staff and several devils were assigned to "take care" of Rachel and Esther, who were involved in the failure of Moloch's operation. Ruben escaped, but it was practically an accident.

Esther and Rachel were of two minds about the future. Rachel apparently still thought it was possible that Joseph would repudiate his betrothed and take up with Esther. The latter was much more astute in that regard. What to do with them? They had served our plan but had not been successful. It was decided that the two of them should be induced to hate each other to the point of death.

The devil Chozeba was charged with the duty. His name, "Liar," indicates all there was to the operation. He began by appearing to Rachel as a man who had had difficulty at Esther's Inn. Said difficulty was the interest its proprietress took in his person. He said that now he had heard that Ruben was the object of Esther's attentions. Rachel was shocked. But then that shock turned to an attitude very typical of humans. She decided that she should have known better than to try to help the other. Her husband seemed to use every excuse to stay away from home, alleging that more men wanted more time studying at the synagogue, which only made her suspicions beautifully worse. But she knew she controlled Ruben.

She would make sure she kept Ruben in line. He was such an idiot; he probably wouldn't even know that Esther was trying to steal his heart. *What a heart, that she should steal it!* After all, she had chosen this man as her best option in dreary old Nazareth. His inadequacy had a way of reflecting back at her that made her uncomfortable.

Meanwhile, Esther had always seemed to her a little too eager to consider herself Rachel's equal. Obviously, she might have more money, but certainly not social standing. That was probably why Joseph had not been moved to make a wrong situation right. He saw no alternative but to do the noble thing. The overeager Esther had spoiled the whole thing. *She didn't deserve Joseph, really.*

Chozeba had rightly estimated that the friendship of the two women was vulnerable to the discovery of their true feelings about each other. Their affection did not exclude feelings of superiority, each feeling superior to the other. Rachel felt that she was Esther's patroness, a social superior who was condescending to help the other. Condescension does not work in a friendship, although, as some wag put it, it is the soundest basis of a relationship. Feeling sorry for friends is a human way of relating. The clodlings seek out relationships of neediness and then pretend that they represent—that dread word—love.

Esther also felt superior to Rachel. Chozeba thus went to her as a merchant who was selling cloth and pretended that Ruben had bought some very nice products that were not destined for his wife. He told her that the leader of the synagogue had given a servant a present. This was based on a real situation. A girl, quite aggressively stupid (something to remember, human ignorance does not automatically translate into humility), had needed another veil because the one she generally wore had holes in it. Ruben had decided to buy her a new veil. A local vendor did not have the cheap material from which the old veil had been made and Ruben had been forced to buy a more expensive one. Normally, this would have been taken care of by Rachel, but there had been tension between herself and the servant at the time. This made the young girl reluctant to approach her mistress about the veil. And so, she had asked Ruben to buy one, or give her the money to do so.

Of course, the servant was never trusted with much money herself, so Ruben decided to buy the cloth himself. Thus far, the truth. However, when Chozeba was telling the (true) story of the purchase, he added details that were incriminating. The veil cost more than Ruben wanted to pay. This was reinterpreted as: he wanted to buy the best for the young woman. Even though the man had barely touched the cloth, his fingers had brushed against it. This was expressed as anxiety about the quality, as if he were already imagining the headdress on a beloved. Then, too, Ruben had called the girl over once the price was settled and gestured to the cloth, indicating "mission accomplished." But Chozeba had him glancing at the girl hoping for approbation. Esther was gifted with the kind of imagination that connected all the innuendo together like one of those childish drawings human use to teach their progeny numbers, the pencil line goes from 1 to 2 to 3 and a pathetic little drawing comes out. The same principle is behind the vision of constellations among the gaseous fires about the universe [Gaseous fires = stars. –Informant]

Immediately, Esther's compassion for Rachel came to the fore. Perhaps this was helped by feelings of envy, which are very strong in all humans. She had been envious of Rachel and her domesticity. Ruben was always around, and seemed so docile. Now, the idea that Ruben was perhaps unfaithful—even if this was only on the level of his imagination—consoled Esther tremendously. At least she did not have to worry about such a thing. *Poor Rachel,* she thought, *and Ruben appeared to be such a different type of man.*

The two women met, then, with very different agendas. Rachel felt that she must signal her dissatisfaction with Esther so that the latter could learn more humility. The two sides of the humility in question were that she should be humbler with Rachel and less confident with herself, especially with the weaker sex. [The devils are onto something there. Men are the weaker ones. –ed.]

Esther had decided not to indicate in any way that she knew that Ruben might have a wandering eye. This resolution was jettisoned almost immediately, as most intentions of guarding secrets are among humans.

The meeting of the two women was carefully guided by Chozeba. First, Rachel gave off an air of indifference at the visit of her friend. She was hoping to convey to Esther that the latter needed her much more than the other way around. This was promptly misunderstood by Esther, who concluded that her friend was depressed because she had discovered Ruben's "interest" in the servant girl.

When Esther said, "I know what you are going through. My husband also had a roving eye," she startled Rachel a great deal.

"What are you trying to say?"

"Nothing, I am your friend. You can be honest with me."

"I am honest. You are imagining things. What makes you insinuate something so patently false?"

This led to Esther's recounting of her conversation with the cloth merchant. Now it happened that Rachel had noticed the new veil that same day. She had been about to comment upon it when she remembered that she was unhappy with the servant girl and did not feel like talking to her. When Esther told her the story, Rachel desperately tried to remember what the girl's veil looked like. Since Ruben never had any interest in what she wore, she assumed that it was perfectly logical that he would care about the servant's girl's veil. She figured that Esther's jealousy of the girl had to do with her own shameless designs on Ruben.

In the midst of their conversation, Chozeba made the servant think she heard her mistress calling for her. She arrived on the scene a bit breathless, which made some color come into her cheeks. The veil looked new to her and Esther made the fateful error of commenting upon it. This made the girl blush, and incensed Rachel. Immediately, she sent the girl away.

Right at that moment, Chozeba had inspired Ruben to return home and meet the two women. Of course, he met the servant girl first, who, surprised to see him, asked him if he needed anything. She was a voluble type, this servant, and it sounded as though she was only too happy to be engaged in the master's service. The exchange was audible where the two women were seated glaring at each other in another part of the house. It was a perfect game for Chozeba.

Esther and Rachel never spoke to each other again in their lives. Rachel had been convinced that Esther had been right, and that made her hate her all the more. She felt betrayed at the very core of her being by her erstwhile friend who had dared to feel compassion for her. As to Ruben, things were smoothed over when the servant girl was sent to her parents, who married her off rapidly to a camel driver who won her heart with his ridiculous ways.

The servant's younger sister—much more shy and more profoundly ignorant—took over the post at the home of Ruben and Rachel.

There have been some who suggested that the friendship of the two women might have been useful when Miriam and Joseph—and, of course, their "child"—came back to Nazareth after the sojourn in exile. In other words, it was a mistake to cause the two to be alienated. This implies that the only resources we had in the forsaken and pathetic little town were Esther and Rachel. There were always other alternatives, and meanwhile we were able to make life a living anticipation of hell for the two ladies, who could neither forget nor forgive each other.

CHAPTER SEVENTEEN: THE ENEMY TAKES ADVANTAGE OF OUR TROOPS

[The author of this document seems almost human in his attention to theological detail and, despite his pompous style, somewhat accurate, if one eliminates the bias. –ed.]

The absolute failure of the operation to sabotage the meeting between Miriam and her cousin Elizabeth has been a source of controversy for many years. I shall lay out the main lines of the two positions on the issue, without taking any stand. The encounter between the future Messiah and the future Precursor was obviously a key element of the Invasion, although our scholars are still trying to understand what happened.

The meeting between the two pregnant women was another disaster for our forces. But this was not because we were caught unaware. The devils had concentrated their forces around the miserable village. There were many of the enemy in the area, but perhaps not so many as we expected at first. Perhaps there was a ratio of two angels to one devil. This still left us with the advantage of a home field and the wonderful debility of the humans. Their propensity to egoism and to "letting themselves go"—as they put it quaintly—is our greatest ally.

Miriam and Joseph descended from Galilee very swiftly. The caravan was extremely well-guarded by the Enemy—the guards were all Thrones, which we thought a bit much. In fact, the thing appeared to be more a procession than a march. There was an extraordinary feel to the exercise, as though it were a triumphal entry to take possession of the land. The irony of these two beggars, one on foot and the other on a pathetic donkey, hurrying the whole way, in fact, sleeping under the stars twice to avoid entering Samaritan cities and at the same time the extraordinary supernatural vigilance of an entire spiritual army invisible about them was, frankly, disconcerting. It was, of course, part of the style of the Invasion. There were two levels: the material, marked by extreme poverty and lack of appearances; and the spiritual, a disproportionate extreme of supernatural presence and gifts.

The gap between the human reality of these poor pilgrims and the spiritual one is what perhaps prevented the sabotage of the operation. Our troops were quite prepared for Miriam's entry into the house at Ein Karem.

Zachary had been prepared. He was still deaf and dumb because of his argument with Gabriel, and it was hoped that his resentment could be played upon by our forces. His unconscious—that treasured human feature for us—was fed with all sorts of suspicions of Miriam and Joseph. A little biography here is helpful. Zachary's status in the world had not risen, and he was less well-off than his parents, who were less well-off than theirs (this could be multiplied by 10 because they had been sinking socially since the times of the Maccabees). Nevertheless, he still had the memory and the pride of better days. Humans are like that; they can take an absurd pride in what their ancestors have lost. It is as if... [This part of the manuscript was censored, perhaps because it referred to angels before the Luciferan uprising. Devils cannot bear to think of that time and do everything to blot out its memory. –Informant]

What we really need at this time, we suggested to the priest, *is not more people involved in this affair. Our only hope according to Elizabeth would be help from Anne and Joachim and their daughter. We have not even heard a word from them in years. They are probably dead; they went off to God-forsaken Galilee. If they are alive, they are probably so poor that they would be a burden on us, not a support. Elizabeth needs help, especially since she decided, apparently, to keep all this secret. Each day the old woman looks worse. It doesn't matter: She will probably lose the child. How could anyone expect that she could have a child at this point in her life!*

This stream of doubts did not have the desired effect on Zachary, who was often to be found outside the house, facing the direction of the detested Temple of Jerusalem, praying. His personal bodyguard (our guard, not the other one!) had to listen to the prayers and it was a painful experience. Zachary had taken refuge in the piety of his youth, and would recite psalms under the stars with a relish that was excruciating.

It was thought that something could be done with the neighbors. However, the couple had withdrawn from social life to some extent. The neighbors didn't even know that the woman was pregnant. Or rather some knew, and others believed what we were putting out, that the woman *thought* she was pregnant. Some were thinking that it was a tumor and the poor girl was going to have the greatest disappointment of her life as she lay dying. Perhaps the agents had spent too much time and effort on such fantasies. They did not prevent the main event—a surprise attack by the Enemy who had only seemed on the defensive.

HSM had been monitoring everything very carefully. We had three divisions in Ein Karem and we waited for the encounter between the two couples. Of course, that was part of the problem. One whole division was supervising Zachary and another was prepared for Joseph. Members of the other group were dispersed among malicious neighbors. It was thought that the two men were our best chance to derail the invasion plans. If they would do something about the situation, it was considered, we would be able to prevent the worst.

What was not expected was a surprise attack involving the women. As soon as they got near each other, our troops were overpowered. By concentrating on the men, they had erred catastrophically. There were signs, of course, but our warriors were not ready. Both Elizabeth and Miriam were surrounded with detachments of angels from the other side. That was a warning, but those on the ground, so to speak, neglected to see that the women were the main draw of the show, and not the two men.

In retrospect, it was certainly a key element that Elizabeth had awakened that day with a great sense of expectation. She had no way of knowing that Miriam was approaching, at least no human, half-clod way of perceiving it. This is another obvious way that the Triune Tyranny operates undercover and in a sneaky and dissembling way. This woman knew "in her heart" that this day was going to be important. How would the wretched woman have known that without a direct intervention by a superior being? Unfair, as usual—the Other Side takes advantage of our adherence to decent standards of fairness. [Malarkey –ed.]

Miriam was coming along at quite a pace, in what one of our agents, not immune to self-serving exaggeration, called "a blinding brilliance, a luminous epiphany, the so-called unbearable light of Otherness when it is manifest in a Creation which really by now belongs to us." (That devil ended up working with the people who write racy Harlequins). Joseph was walking beside the inevitable donkey rapt in his own prayers. The donkey itself seemed to be aware of the importance of rushing to the encounter with Elizabeth. Imagine a superior being investing dumb animals with an awareness of supernatural realities! It really is undignified.

Elizabeth caught sight of Miriam and immediately there was a kind of spiritual earthquake in the world. A whirlwind of the Third Person of the Pretender Triumvirate [a relatively little-used formula for the Holy Spirit – Informant] engulfed the wretched woman and she began to spout the awful incoherence of the profligate and irresponsible mixing of the divinity with humanity. Specifically, Elizabeth hailed her young cousin and pronounced her "blessed among women."

We have had some luck making even followers of the Great Pretender *Who-Would-Be-King* of this world to reject any title for his mother. By dint of constantly repeating our attack on her, we have been able to convince even some of the most pious wretches to deprecate the role of the woman who made possible the Invasion of the world. If the Son is important precisely because he has combined the Divine with the human, the mother has to be seen as key. However, humans are inconsistent in the application of their ideas, and some think that by disparaging the mother they praise the son. In the human mind the absurd is tolerated. That is one of our secret weapons.

"And blessed is the fruit of thy womb," said the horrible woman. That prayer has caused us so much torture and frustration that I need not comment about it other than to say what an extraordinarily vulgar and low way to behave that a Spiritual being *par excellence* should be described as being "fruit" of a "womb." How absolutely appalling the mixture of Creator-created, spirit-matter, rationality-absurdity!

The greeting had our troops howling in pain, to use the picturesque speech of the half-clods, but worse was to come. The old woman Elizabeth proclaimed that her child also felt the presence of Miriam and her child. "Who am I that the mother of my Lord should come to me?" This has often been described as a prayer of great humility. I would say it refers to the great *humiliation* of the Spirit that would enter defective matter, wedding itself for all eternity with what has been demonstrated not to fulfill spiritual expectations. When the hag pronounced these words, several devils started reeling back and did not stop until they reached the desert of Sinai. This first example of devotion to the mother of the Great Pretender was the harbinger of a history of unseemly attacks on us by means of the same.

"My child leapt for joy at the sound of your voice," said Elizabeth to Miriam. As much as we would like the humans to forget that the child in the womb is a sentient, independent being, it leaks out sometimes that the fetus actually hears what goes on outside the walls of the womb and even reacts to certain things. Lucky for us, a hedonistic age can ignore such data or Moloch would not be as important as he is in the Infernal Court.

As if all of this were not disgusting enough, worse was yet to come. Miriam was to reply to the greeting of her cousin with the words that have done such damage to us. There are still benighted masses in places on earth that carry about the words of Miriam as some kind of spiritual token. Their *Magnificat* in their purses and wallets, they feel, protects against us, just because that prayer drives us to the edge of impotence. In a separate appendix I will analyze this supposed "prayer of protection" even though many have told me that it is dangerous even to pay attention to such things.

CHAPTER EIGHTEEN:
THE INFAMOUS PRAYER

[Appears to be some kind of study aid. Heavily censored in the original, like government documents released in the United States by means of so-called Freedom of Information appeals, with all the really good information blotted out. –Informant]

You have all probably heard of the prayer, but it is useful sometimes to vaccinate with the same ugly infection in order immunize the system, to use a half-clod metaphor regarding praxis with certain diseases on earth. For that reason, I append this exercise, and not as some kind of defeatist or Michaelist infiltration technique, although my enemies may spit whatever accusation against me.

[I have supplied the censored verses. –ed. **"My soul proclaims the greatness of the Lord"**]

This odious phrase is exactly what we want to teach the half-clods *not* to do. We want them to be wrapped up in *themselves* and not think of the Other or really any other thing except in terms of their own pleasure or sense of well-being.

[**"My spirit rejoices in God my Savior"**]

The complete unjust, illogical, and inexplicable favoritism of the Trinitarian Tyranny is revealed in this line. A half-clod's "spirit," certainly not the noblest thing in creation, is "rejoicing" because the TT has decided to "save" it. What spiritual being would bother about such a miserable half-breed thing like the human race!

["**For He has looked with favor on His lowly servant**"]

Most human "humility" is fake, a rhetorical device to call attention to the speaker. Unfortunately, this was not the case with Miriam, who never seemed to "get" her exalted position and thus was impervious to all our attempts to make her sin by pride. Even when her son had to do things that preoccupied her and upset her, she showed the most despicable docility.

["**From this day all generations will call me blessed**"]

We have done our best in this regard to make sure there is always dissonance on this subject. There was a terrible time for more than a thousand years when every follower of the Pretender showed affection and respect for his mother, but that changed about one thousand five hundred years after His death. It is nevertheless remarkable that the young woman could have a keen insight into how others would see her in history without the corresponding pride natural to such knowledge. Another logical anomaly in the almost incredible series of absurdities that we know of as the Invasion.

["**The Almighty has done great things for me and holy is His name**"]

Two objections: 1. How "almighty" can He be if we are allowed to run about as we please? 2. The ["holiness of His

Name?"] [This part was irrecoverable. –Informant]

["**He has mercy on all who fear Him in every generation**"]

This phrase seems to be "full of positive feelings," as some of the half-clods would say, but we can always insist that we do not need his mercy.

["**He has shown the strength of His arm, He has scattered the proud in their conceit**"]

As usual, there is a reference to His omnipotence, "which he uses sparingly with us" as the old joke says. Then the reference to pride. That the TT would feel it necessary in this kind of a conversation to bring up our "difference of opinion" with us is typical. We may be proud, according to the lights of the *Ancien Regime*, as His Satanic Majesty calls it, but we are hardly scattered. We are everywhere. "If we are scattered, let us make the most of it." How can the TT talk about our conceit, when there are so many conceited humans, pieces of clay who pretend to such importance in the universe just because...? [This part was deleted by Hell's censors, perhaps because the devils don't want to be reminded of the Incarnation? – Informant]

["**He has cast down the mighty from their thrones and has lifted up the lowly**"]

One of the ironies of the absurd politics of the TT is the constant prejudice that is evinced against the powerful. Is it our fault that we are much greater than these pieces of clay He has taught to dance and to weep? Throughout all the propaganda of the so-called Ancient Covenant, there is always the capricious turning of tables. [The original refers to a spiritual gyre that is too complicated to explain. –Informant] Some group gets power, and then when it begins to use it, is suddenly cut off. The poor and lowly are such because they are innately inferior. That is why we dominate this kingdom. Hail Satan, etc.

["**He has filled the hungry with good things and the rich he has sent away empty**"] Here is the plan of our enemy. He wants to break our hold over the persons who have need and therefore are angry and of those who have all they want. Because the rich are a "law unto themselves" we are able to do well with them.

["**He has come to the help of His servant Israel, for He has remembered His promise of mercy, the promise he made to our fathers, to Abraham and his children forever**"]

Here Miriam was repeating the propaganda she no doubt learned at the feet of her parents, Joachim and Anna. Two half-clods who were favored by the Enemy in outrageous ways—Jacob, aka Israel; the father of children by four women who limped his way into history; a dreamer of dreams, who ran away from his idiot and lazy brother—and Abraham, the dreamer's grandfather, who withheld nothing from the TT, according to reports. If only we could have done a Job number on that Abraham, perhaps we could have shaken off his dreadful attachment to the Tyranny. But he was stupid enough to say "whatever" every time he was asked to give up what little he had. You have a home, "leave it"; you have something in the hand, a dream of a life, "throw it away"; you have a son, "give him back to me." And all the while the man goes on cheerfully giving thanks, groveling and offering sacrifices. Who would have predicted that he would be more important than men who made empires, constructed pyramids, made their names resound the orb?

CHAPTER NINETEEN:
THE MENDAX GAMBIT

[The catty historian continues. –Informant. A colorful description, at least. –ed.]

By the end of the young woman's words, our troops were in disarray. If we were half-clods, we would have been holding our hands over our ears, because of this terrible attack *by a means quite unexpected*. That is always the secret weapon of the Enemy, using weapons we least expect.

Retreat was sounded and the devils all left the scene. When HSM found out, he was of course incensed against the stupidity of leaving the field to the enemy. However, he decided that this incident was only a battle. "One may lose many battles and yet win the war," he said. The troops on the ground were immediately transferred to "guarding prisoners." [This is apparently a reference to a tour of duty in hell. It seems that nothing disgusts the devils more than "guarding" the condemned. –Informant]

The Invasion continued unhampered. Joseph and Miriam returned to Nazareth. In the three months that had lapsed there had been some changes in the little town.

Esther and Rachel had paid the price of their inutility. The first had been married to a ne'er do well, a drunkard and a retainer from Herod's court who was hell-bent "to run through Esther's money" [There followed here an expression that only devils understand, presumably ironic. – Informant], the half-clods said (ironically, really, because they could not have known). Of course, ignorance does not appear to be a condition that prevents them from holding forth on all manner of topics. The husband's name was Jethro.

Rachel meanwhile had developed a tumor in her stomach. The half-clods have a strange weakness. Their organs of assimilating matter to maintain their bodies often malfunction because of psychic reasons. They are frustrated in something, their digestion fails. Or they are resentful, a tumor starts growing. Obviously, the Psychosomatic Institute of Hell has banks of data on these things, but it cannot be entirely explained to us. How does the spirit part cause the material part to suffer in specific ways? What we know is that it does, sometimes, but not always. Rachel worried a tumor into development somewhere in those messy midsections humans have and passed away even before Miriam and Joseph even returned. Esther sometimes thought that Rachel had been luckier than she. Her "tumor" slept late in the morning and was always looking for more expensive wines. Elementary mathematics escaped him, so he saw no problem in spending more than was coming in from the business Esther ran so astutely.

I expatiate on this subject because this husband of Esther, Jethro, was under the influence of Mendax, an angel of mediocre talents. This Mendax played the idiot human for all that he was worth. Esther eventually was tempted to kill the man. He had put on weight; he was constantly winking at the housemaids, almost always failing to grope them, but because he was drunk, not from not trying his worst. He invited friends to bacchanals, and he offended practically everyone in the small town, including the officers who occasionally visited there. It was a *tour de force* by Mendax. Esther's suffering when she saw Joseph and Miriam return was wonderful. All the agents in Nazareth considered Mendax a genius.

He was too clever by half, however. [Some kind of favorite expression in these pages, making me wonder if the Informant used it frequently. – ed.] Sometimes you can overdo a bad thing. By concentrating so much on Esther's punishment and Jethro's outrageous behavior, valuable resources were wasted. This was not realized until later at Mendax's trial, when Prosecutor Faucus, speaking for HSM, pointed out very clearly that the devil had missed opportunities to wreak havoc because he was too interested, and invested too much time and energy, in a loser whom we would have been able to win without so much flair. It is a besetting fault of some devils that they are so showy. Efficiency would do us much better. But no, some of the finest talents have to try to make a name for themselves with extravagance. No teamwork, everyone wants his own trophies. How many times have we lost souls because of a simple lack of coordination?

The "*no soy marinero, soy capitán*" tendency, which has been associated with the Michaelist heresy has demonstrated that an *embarrass de mal* spoils the atmosphere. The art of damnation requires some restraint. There are people who would lose their souls for a new car or a trip to the Caribbean and some devils are busy working up terrorist plots and helping serial murders. Suburbia is a more fertile field for our work than other places because there you find many cold hearts and false belief. A cocktail party in a gated community can sometimes make for real gains that outdistance those possible at an atheist's convention.

Mendax tried for effects that indicated more interest in making noise than in substantive achievements. Certainly, this angel had a certain reputation in academic circles and was preferred for his job instead of more worthy devils. He was the favorite of a certain... [Again, the manuscript was heavily censored. Perhaps Mendax had been restored to favor and it was impolitic to criticize him so strongly, or higher-ups were implicated in the criticism. The Politburo of Hell has some complicated movements and a lot of recycling goes on. –Informant]

Esther was able to appreciate the cruelty of her punishment because she was able one day to see Joseph, very content, walking with Miriam near the market. Her husband Jethro was, as usual, at the establishment of a certain seller of wines, and the formidable Esther was on her way to rebuke the wine seller and threaten never to buy from him again if he let her husband get drunk on his premises. This was not the first time that Nazareth had seen a public outburst by the woman. She was very angry, the veins on her half-clod neck protruding with emotion, and then she encountered the two of them.

Of course, she was taken aback. Miriam was "showing," as the earthlings say. And Joseph had a serenity about him that was practically palpable. "The old cuckold," thought Esther, with a little prompting of her devil guardian. Then the eyes of the two women met. It was another case of the tricks of the Enemy. Esther melted under the gaze of the girl. We are not sure exactly what Miriam communicated by a mere glance, but her older rival instantly flushed red in the face and turned around and went home.

The wine seller would get his punishment the next day when she refused the barrels he sent over, but he was not to receive the public humiliation she had planned. He came to Esther's inn fawning all over the place, and the woman was cold as ice with him. She did not deign even to tell him why she had purchased the wine she needed from the man's chief rival. Her silence made the man feel worse, because he immediately suspected that someone had told Esther of what he had been saying about her and Jethro. That would complicate his relationship with Jethro, also, whom he mocked without pity. He was quite abashed by the whole thing. Mendax thought it a special touch to make all the wine in the barrels Esther did not buy go sour. The man was practically ruined. But that is an example of an achievement that distracted needed attention from the Invasion.

Even worse was the aneurism Mendax engineered for Jethro, which left him totally helpless. Thus, Esther at the end of the game had a husband who could not speak with her and with whom she did not want to speak. Loneliness à *deux* is how Mendax described her fate. But this was also a diversion. It was not necessary to spend so much energy on the damned couple.

[A hellish footnote accompanied this text, which I reprint here: "And I say damned unfortunately only in an analogous way (I speak like a theologian) because both of these half-clods ended up in Purgatory. We think Esther did because of a gold coin she pressed into Joseph's hand when he did some minor work at the inn, overpaying the man. With Jethro, there was a lapse in vigilance. It was thought that his embittered state would hold up through the dying process. Nevertheless, the old man was able to survive more than five earth 'years' and see the Child of Mary when the 'family' returned to Nazareth for what we call the Great Hiatus, the *Sitz Krieg* of 18 years between his furtive attempt to teach in the Temple and the ministry he commenced at thirty years old when the Great Pretender did nothing. Apparently, Jethro smiled at the boy-deity and was rewarded by the grace of repentance. Another criminal caprice by the Trinitarian Tyranny. The man had certainly merited eternal condemnation." - Informant]

As Mendax was doing his pirouettes of malice, Joseph and Mary settled down to a very quiet life. Then, of course, the days became short for the infamous trip to Bethlehem. With extraordinary perspicuity for a human, Joseph arranged that his in-laws would be cared for while he was gone. Supposedly the time would only be a few months. At least that is the impression he gave to Joachim and Anna. The transcripts show evasive language, but no outright lies, and we have gone over them very studiously. The old people were provided for and eventually would see their "grandchild," albeit briefly. Both were dead within a year of the Invader's relocation to Nazareth, but such matter does not interest us here.

In the next chapter I will deal with the circumstances of the infamous Birth of the Messiah. Since my interest is technical, I will not enter into all philosophic implications but will only talk about tactics that were used and why they were eventually proved to be unsuccessful. This study might seem to some to be "a useless repeating of errors, chewing the cud of strategic mistakes" as one of my "colleagues" has stated in a not-so-secret memorandum. However, I appeal to HSM to silence the perverse critic because it was on HSM's orders that I undertook to prepare this summary of the first part of the Invasion History, the part that was for all of us so difficult and painful.

CHAPTER TWENTY:
THE FOOLPROOF PLAN, PART ONE

[This author speaks such official-ese "truth-spinning" that the devil must have been part of the infernal bureaucracy. –Informant; Bit of a redundancy there, I'm afraid. It does represent a great deal of "doth protest too much." –ed.]

Among those of the despicable Michaelist tendencies, there has been some secret discussion of the failure of the infallible plan endorsed by His Satanic Majesty for the murder of Number Two, aka "The Pretender of Bethlehem."

First of all, it is most important that it be understood that HSM did not make a mistake. [Please note that the devil forgets to have a "second" to this "first." Interesting error for a supposedly superior being. – ed.] Those close to him may have been too optimistic, but he himself never makes mistakes. With that principle in mind, it will be easier to understand the failure of the First Assassination Attempt. It will be clear to all that the steps taken at the birth of the Pretender to the Throne of the World led ultimately to a successful termination, although after a hiatus of thirty-three years.

The "Plan" as it was called was not elaborated by HSM

himself but by the then satrap Starkstern. It consisted in various elements and contingencies. If element A of the plan did not work there was always element B, and, if not, element C. One strategy might make another unnecessary, but they were supposed to anticipate all possible outcomes. [This is one of the few parts of the manuscript that the Informant abbreviated, because the devilish author went through the whole Hebrew Alphabet, from aleph to taw. –ed.]

The details of the failure of the first part of the plan have been well known to us but not to the half-clods. Still, it is worthy of at least a summary treatment. The interested reader may look to the Archives for a more detailed history.

The essence of the first phase of the Plan was to make the "delivery" of the Pretender as difficult as possible. Thus, the Romans were moved to make a census, causing a great movement of peoples around Palestine, and many visitors to Bethlehem. This was done so surreptitiously that there was no record left in Roman archives. That was because it was a whim of the Governor of Syria, who was *de facto* governor before being *de jure*, which has stood us in good stead with the scholars we call the Doubters. (The Doubters are the erudite readers of the Bible who insist on systematic skepticism about everything that is in the book. They actually take mythology more seriously than their supposed field of expertise. One of many successes we have had with Academia).

Then there was the "no room at the inn" gambit. This was easy to do once all the Bethlehemites were required to go back to their miserable village. The weather was favorable to us, also. We had hoped that the boy would "catch his death of cold," a clodling saying.

When Joseph and Miriam arrived in Bethlehem, a light snow was falling. As we had planned, not one of the traveler's lodges accepted them. Let me explain what was done, because, although it was not entirely successful, the plot was ingenious.

A day before Miriam and Joseph were to arrive in Bethlehem, we arranged that the innkeepers would not be friendly to them. We did this by sending in a scouting party of devils who worked with admirable efficiency. I will quote directly from the reports made to the Infernal Archives:

When we arrived in Bethlehem, we immediately looked up one of our I.O.U.s that was hanging on death's door. [An "I.O.U." is apparently a miserable wretch who has promised his soul to the devil in exchange for some earthly benefit. –Informant] Beraka was the man for us, oddly named for blessing. He lived in Adullam, just a few miles away from Bethlehem, but at enough a distance that he was unknown there. Beraka had promised us his soul in exchange for cheating his brother of an inheritance.

His elder brother Jonathan had been forced to flee because of accusations of a murder perpetrated by Beraka himself. What the poor fool did not know was that the Enemy had actually chosen Jonathan for another mission. The latter had fled to the enormous (bigger than Palestine's) community of the Chosen People in Egypt. There he had been quite successful. Jonathan began working for a man who sold cattle. This man was a Jew without family. His wife had died at a young age, followed by their children. He was quite disappointed in life and embittered to the extent that his devil guard neglected him. When Jonathan came on the scene the disgusting half-clod conceived a real love for him. He helped him pick out a wife, the daughter of one of his cousins, and eventually made Jonathan the heir of all his possessions. This was all part of the Enemy's plan, because sometime later Jonathan was to become the host of Joseph, Miriam and the Pretender to the Throne of this World. The deviousness of our Enemy, taking one of our "victims"—this brother of Beraka—and making him a key part of the Invasion plans is only another example of how we should be prepared for "anything" from You Know Who.

Fortunately, Beraka never found out about his brother Jonathan before we whisked him off to perpetual incarceration. He had the impression that he had his brother's blood on his hands, because we had several times planted rumors to that effect in Bethlehem. Now, Beraka was at the end of the life granted him by *You Know Who*. He was dying of cirrhosis but was in total denial about it. We suggested to him that he "pretend" to be mortally ill with the plague and that a good revenge on this unhappy world would be to scare all those who came into contact with him. He was so embittered, he loved the idea.

We convinced him that he should say that he had just come from Nazareth and that he was fleeing an outbreak of the plague. There was a real actor in him and he was thrilled to have a role that would gain him a great deal of attention. Somehow the idiot was convinced that it was in his interest to disparage the people from Nazareth. Some devils were even surprised that he had heard of the place. He would get to the Inn, tell his story and stay one night. Then he was to move on. At least that was what he thought was going to happen.

In actual fact, he went into one of the more popular establishments in Bethlehem. By "popular" I mean it as the half-clods sometimes do, "cheap." Beraka had been instructed to make the "news" of the plague outbreak in Nazareth as public as possible. Thus, he was shouting—the wretch always shouted—to the innkeeper in front of a good group of clients and those who attended them. These included those who groomed horses and donkeys and kept them for the guests. This particular set of people is great at communicating gossip, since they go from inn to inn.

Beraka "waxed eloquent," as the half-clods say, about how glad he was to get out of Galilee. We had to admire the man's gusto for lying. "Is there anyone here from Nazareth?" he asked in a spooky voice, his eyes dancing macabrely about his face. "Good then, maybe we're safe. I will not stay where anyone from Nazareth stays. The plague has broken out in that disgusting village. They die a terrible death those who catch it, if you know what I mean, which I hope you do, because it is not in our interest to get infected with that curse of the -------. [Censored, best guess is that the devils don't want to use the word "almighty." –Informant]

In the middle of his recounting of the horrors of the plague and how he wanted to avoid it, Beraka began coughing. This was followed by severe bleeding. [Here you will miss a valuable nuance that I have not been able to translate from angelspeak. Apparently, the devils have an obsession with blood, or as they call it, the "vital fluid." The Informant confessed to me that the way the devils speak of bloodletting is "two parts" pleasure and "two parts" disgust, and "all parts" intensity...as only angels can be intense. I told him that I thought this had to do with the Precious Blood of Our Savior, an idea which appealed to the Informant, in spite of the fact that his theological knowledge was a bit spotty, because he said it just made sense to him. -ed.]

The half-clod I.O.U. expired in a pool of his own blood in front of the innkeeper, the servants, and—most important of all—the groomsmen from the local stables. Everyone was horrified, of course. His corpse was thrown on the back of a broken-down donkey and taken out to the place where the town disposed of their garbage. The workers did not even save the cloth that covered the body, it was too disgusting for them to rescue. They were a couple of drunks and they were paid in wine for their duty. Perhaps because they were so drunk, they considered themselves immune to the plague. However, others did not consider them that way and they were eventually chased out of town by a group of thugs with clubs.

The whole show was wonderfully successful. The groomsmen practically chased each other around town to tell the bad news. That is another great resource for us, the *Schadenfreude* [The devil knows German, of course, but not many people where I live, so I give the translation "joy at the misery of another." -ed.] of the typical half-clod. They have a sort of taste for bad news. Their brains show the materiality that clouds their intelligences by seeking always emotion and the sensational. Many who are meek as mice will gorge themselves on the details of the latest murder. One can look into any numbers of homes and see a collection of persons around the television set, attracted to whatever is on like so many filaments of iron to a magnet.

Those who pander to the "taste of the tasteless"—as one of our more waggish devils has called it—are successful half-clods who compete in telling stories of gore and betrayal. The whole thing represents a very fertile field for us. There is apparently no point too low in human conduct to serve as a topic of conversation or theme for personal meditation. Even we are surprised sometimes by the attitude of the half-clods. Their imagination makes them wallow about a good deal, like those animals [swine –ed.] that serve them for food and cool themselves off snuggling into the mud.

So, everyone in town heard about the plague victim from Nazareth. The story appealed to another aspect of *Schadenfreude* that half-clods are fond of. The man fleeing the plague already has it. What you do to avoid something only draws you near to it. For some reason that sort of thing has an attraction for half-clods. They grasp their freedom so poorly that they are mostly fatalists at heart. This even applies to the religious ones; John Calvin is an example. Half-clods have a love-hate relationship with their moral freedom (along with everything else). [Interesting how the devil seems to corroborate what I learned about Calvin in Maynooth. –ed.]

But enough of philosophizing. Beraka's demise scared all the innkeepers in Bethlehem. Actually, there were not so many formal inns in the Podunk little town. People would take in travelers on an individual basis. That is why it was crucial to connect "Nazareth" with "Plague." It was a complete success.

Joseph went from inn to inn and home to home. His own relatives did not take compassion on him. All he had to do was say that he had come from Nazareth and panic seized the hearers. Instantly, the half-clods would change their perspective—such is the power of a prejudice well planted. We were all very content. Everything was set for the Pretender to be born in the streets of Bethlehem, in the chill that we had also been able to arrange. The devils sensed Joseph's mounting anxiety, even though he tried to show a brave face to Miriam. He acted as if all was according to plan. We thought for a moment that it was according to *our* plan, but that proved slightly overoptimistic. [The devil is usually very fond of euphemisms—hence: "slightly overoptimistic." -Informant]

CHAPTER TWENTY-ONE:
NATHAN

[A podcast style. – Informant]

Miriam was already in labor when the pair bumped into Nathan. [The careful reader will remember that he was the man who fled from his servitude and feigned leprosy, passing through Nazareth and meeting Miriam in the street. –ed.]

Again, our Enemy had staged the whole maneuver. There is no use even analyzing the injustice of the move. A miserable wretch escapes slavery and then somehow "bumps into"—a half-clod phrase—the Mother-To-Be of Number 2? The whole thing is beyond parody. Half-clods build up relationships on the basis of mere accidents. So, you met this useless piece of animate matter while he was escaping for his life pretending to have a disease that corrodes that matter? The lesson was: Treat him well, because later he will save you when you are wandering homeless, too.

There is a sort of crude understanding of matter that half-clods have, vainly called "science" by them. One of the key precepts of this "science" is that matter is never destroyed; only transformed into some other kind of matter. Some special ones realize that charity is likewise never destroyed; only transformed. It is eternal, and so what one of these miserable wretches does in charity is imperishable. Fortunately for us, very few of them have been able to recognize this truth. [Beautiful thought for a devil. –ed.]

Nathan was the owner of a small property on the outskirts of Bethlehem. Things had not gone so well with him since his return from Damascus. He had a propensity to drink and he was lonely. While he had gained his freedom from his master, and some material security, he had not found happiness. Half-clods are on a constant search for happiness. It drives them the way wind propels sailboats. [I have tried for an equivalent to the angelic metaphor. –Informant; *Indeed?* –ed.] Obviously that *penchant* for happiness is to our advantage, as it makes it easy to manipulate them, particularly when they are hurt, lonely or sick. However, it is a two-edged sword for us, because sometimes the miserable things end up looking to heaven for happiness.

The wretched man made a living from his animals. He had a pair of oxen for plowing that he rented out to farmers, as well as some cows, from whose milk he produced some cheeses, especially the soft kind because it requires little skill. He had one horse and a few asses, also for rent to carry burdens and supplies. He lived in a lean-to shack about a stone's throw from a cave where he kept his animals. His existence was not far removed from that of the animals who gave him his livelihood. In the shack he barely had room to lie down.

He was not the marrying kind in the sense that he

thought he could live alone without becoming too desperate. Some half-clods can no more live alone than other species of mammals. Nathan was extremely lonely. He would have liked to marry, but he had a keen sense of his own unattractiveness. He decided that whoever might want to live with him would do so only out of desire for material advantage. His master had been one of those fools for love we are always looking for. Nathan had observed the difficulties that his master's romantic inclinations had brought him and had decided against it.

Some half-clods are able to forget about their sensual side because of spiritual reasons. With Nathan, a certain fastidiousness militated against him sinning carnally. He regarded prostitutes as unclean and treacherous to the money pouch. His impression of women was that if he ever found one who could capture his heart, it would certainly be a person who would not want to be associated with the likes of him.

He was afflicted with a kind of vestigial but nevertheless noxious spirituality. The ethos of the Essenes seemed to attract him and sometimes he would be in his cups and think about going out to the desert to live with the monks. His interior life was incipient, and sometimes caused a great deal of worry for his guard, but it was an interior life without a center. (Obviously, it is hard for us to deal with people who really know themselves, but there are always ways around that, too.)

The hope of heaven had not yet completely filled the wretched man's consciousness, but it was a recurring motif in his thoughts. His personal devil had to work hard to keep Nathan away from the synagogue and in the taverns. Though the man liked to drink a great deal, and this meant socially, naturally, his personality made it difficult for him to keep friends. He would tire of his fellow-drinkers and inevitably begin to quarrel with them. He would get in arguments about politics, about business, about local personalities, about the hope of Israel, about the rabbis in town, about the principal figures in the social life of the poverty-stricken town they lived in.

He was not completed self-centered, unfortunately, and was capable of some discernment. He recognized, although vaguely, that he, Nathan, was not the axis of importance in the universe, something many drunks are unclear about. They really feel that what happens to them is crucial to the universe. Nathan had his "issues" as half-clods say nowadays, but he had enough sense to be disgusted by querulous persons who were always complaining about life's injustices. Occasionally, he would wax poetic about another possibility of human existence. This was always uncomfortable for his demon guard, because there always existed the danger that he might communicate hope to someone who heard him. Obviously, we appreciate the illusion of hope, but the thing in itself works like poison on our plans.

Nathan's aggressive character and his impatience helped us in this matter, however. Many would not take him seriously, and others feared talking to him. Sometimes at his most lucid moments, and that was often near the end of the barrel of wine, he would say something not only coherent, but really dangerous. Somehow, he had the insight that a key event was about to happen. Several times, he told his fellow oenophiles that he was certain that history would be made in their time. He was suitably mysterious about this and did not mention his encounter with the almost invisible girl, but he made our agents uneasy.

Just one night before the arrival of Joseph and Miriam, Nathan was holding forth to four other men trying to drown their sorrows in fermented grape juice. Perhaps that is one advantage of materiality... [Apparently censored, making it difficult to see how the following fits in the narrative. –Informant]

Of course, materiality has also to do with the way humans behave toward each other. For that reason, the appearance of a half-clod sometimes is his or her destiny. It might even have more far-reaching effects. There is a famous expression of an intellectual who (just barely) escaped our clutches who said that history might have been different if a certain Egyptian queen had had a longer (hence, less attractive) nose.

Because of the above, I will give a description of the material dimension of Nathan. He had sandy-brown hair, thinning, and was slim, with brown eyes that reflected some of the light of day. Half-clods often have an obsession about their organs of vision. They say that they can somehow detect spiritual qualities through looking at the eyes of another person. On the face of it, this is absurd. However, they insist that if one does not look into the eyes of the other, he or she is lying. Also, that some undefined and not materially measurable qualities in the eyes of the other can tell of such virtues as compassion, sincerity, spirituality, love, etc. When people looked into the light brown eyes of Nathan, some thought they saw honesty. Obviously, another mystery (or perhaps mystification) for us of matter mixed up with spirit.

His voice was deep, especially surprising considering

his slight build. When he faced an interlocutor, and locked his eyes on those of his listener, and then spoke with his voice in the lower registers of human audition, there was something compelling in his manner. His skin was light because he avoided the sun with a passion.

"I will tell you something, Enoch," he said to the fellow at his right hand. "There is a girl I have seen. I am convinced she will be the mother of the Messiah."

Enoch nodded his head in drunken acquiescence. He would have done so if Nathan had told him Armageddon was going to happen in three minutes right on the patio of the inn. Two brothers who were also imbibing, Josiah and Hezekiah, looked at Nathan with doubt. They were actually related to the Davidic dynasty—hence their names—and felt that somehow they should know about this. "But you are not of the house of David," protested Josiah. "And know nothing, for a virgin will have the child who is to be the Messiah." This showed that our attempt to make a reasonable interpretation of the one of the prophets, and not insist on *technical* virginity, was not completely successful.

"I know a virgin will bear him," said Nathan with an air that compels attention among the half-clods. They are always a bit put off by someone who claims secret knowledge, but apparently it depends on the tone of voice, too. "I am familiar with the prophecy. But you have not met her, as I have."

"You have met her?" asked the fourth drunk, a certain Solomon. He then lapsed into something like a comatose state. He was followed immediately in this dip into unconsciousness by Enoch. Josiah, remarking on this, said, "Look at them, they are so out of it," and then noticed that his own brother had fallen asleep standing up. "I thought you were going outside," he said to his brother, and then proceeded to the door. He woke up the next day sleeping in a corral for sheep. Nathan remained alone in his intensity.

"Why does this always happen when I am revealing this secret?" the man asked distractedly. The crisis was past, the men would remember nothing the next day and Nathan walked home.

CHAPTER TWENTY-TWO: THE STABLE

Nathan's remark about the Messiah did not escape the notice of his demon custodian. The next day Nathan's devil asked for some support, and three demons followed him around Bethlehem until they regarded it as too boring. Angelic *ennui* is one of our great problems, as HSM has pointed out. Just when we think we have a soul's guaranteed damnation sometimes, there is a moment of carelessness and something happens. In this case, Nathan went about his daily chores, speaking to his groom, arranging the purchase of animal feed, concluding a transaction to sell a white donkey to a very drunk Roman traveler, and it did not seem that even he remembered what he had been speaking about the day before. His personal devil thought that the hungover state would not pose many problems, being one so close to hellishness anyway.

Of course, that was a detail, but our Enemy seizes on such things. When night fell, Nathan was walking down a street in Bethlehem, not sure of which tavern to visit. A vague uneasiness clung to him, as if he were expecting something unfortunate to happen. This was a familiar feeling for him. Unfortunately, at exactly this juncture, his devil decided to take a spin of the town with the other agents. His name will not be mentioned here because he has been reinstated despite his error.

Nathan then met Miriam and Joseph in the street. Joseph immediately addressed himself to him, "Brother, do thou knowest where we can stay this cold night? My wife is about to give birth."

That was typical of the man, so terse and without adornment in speech. Again, this underlines how the multiplication of words suits us. The more these half-clods talk, the better for us. Nathan looked at the man who had spoken to him in the style of the Qumran monks and at first was annoyed. Why was this man talking to him? Half-clods are accustomed to beggars, but Nathan hated them, which was ironic considering his own encounter with Miriam, in which he found himself not only a mendicant, but one whose aspect made everyone fearful of him. He was about to address Joseph sharply when he saw the girl.

"It is you! What are you doing here?"

"My son is to be born this night," said Miriam in a voice that resonated in Nathan's ears as though he were alone in a wind tunnel ["I cannot explain the angelic original which I have translated this way" was the note the Informant had scrawled on this part of the manuscript. – ed.]

"Well, you must go to an inn for travelers. I will pay to have you stay in the best in this village," he said. When he saw that Joseph was shaking his head side to side, which the half-clods do to express disagreement, he asked, "What is it with you, man? Am I not a man of my word?"

Joseph patiently explained to him that they had been

turned away each time they said they were from Nazareth. Nathan himself had heard of the death of our stooge Beraka, and was quick to understand. He himself slept in a shed that was so small he had to lie on his side to fit in with his knees bent.

"All I have is where I keep my animals," he said, as though he were speaking to himself, "At least it will be warm."

The half-clods are sensitive to the temperature (something caused by the speed of the agitation of molecules) of their environment. Hence, of course, the fires of hell—for them. However, in the time the Pretender to the Throne of This World was born there was no such thing as central heating. Hence Nathan was correct about the advantage of the warmth of the animals. In fact, we have seen this circumstance as another example of how the Enemy foiled our plan. If Miriam had given birth in a place where travelers lodged, it would have been more likely for the chill to affect either mother or child. Brute nature conspired against us in the form of the ox and ass and other animals in Nathan's cave. The Creator accepting the help of the most rudimentary of his creations. Another in so many egregious faults of logic and self-respect.

The demonic spies that followed the procession of angels guarding Joseph and Miriam immediately set about trying to foil Nathan's generosity. He began seeing things in his way, first giant ghostly trees to make him afraid of taking the couple through the field to the cave. Then Nathan saw the ground covered by scorpions. He halted for a time on the path, and Joseph had to urge him onwards.

"Don't you see the scorpions?" Nathan asked.

"No, brother, there are in truth no scorpions."

That very moment Nathan could no longer see any of the scorpions. However, the demons made the darkness around the path hiss with the sound of a multitude of serpents. Nathan stopped again, terrified by the noise.

Miriam said to him, "If you will lend us the lantern, we will find our way to the stable."

This served to make Nathan more courageous and they walked the short path to the cave. In a kind of state of ecstasy, he spoke to the animals: "Humankind has not been kind with these people, but you will show them the compassion. Your breath and the heat thrown off by your bodies will keep them warm. All the hospitality denied them by men you will show them in your animal nature. A brute hospitality to life will help them to sleep in this cold. You are creatures of the same Heavenly Father. With wisdom without words, you shall bear witness to the great mystery by which a man is born into this world. Only your radical innocence is worthy of such a sight." What claptrap! Animal compassion, etc. As if we did not know the man's guardian angel was feeding him such lines!

He left the two of them there, filled with a sense of unworthiness to be present at the birth of the child. It was astonishing how the Enemy inspired the man with such uncharacteristic reverence. He practically walked backward to get to the rude shed where he slept at night and he flung himself on a blanket and fell immediately into a deep sleep. Was this sleep natural? He did not wake up for the chanting of the angels or for the visit of the shepherds. It has been alleged that his demon guards had overdone it on having him drink so much wine that evening before.

And so it happened. At the first cry of the *Boy* all the

demons who had gathered near the stable flew off into the night. The locals claimed to have heard the sound of a myriad of bats' wings, but eventually we were able to suppress the tradition. The Invasion had come out into the open, as it were. Here was this supposedly defenseless being, a half-clod babe in swaddling clothes, come to contest our dominion over wretched creation. It is completely understandable that those on guard in Bethlehem would flee with no more idea of what they were doing than to escape the vicinity.

Also understandable is why that legion has been kept in the deepest dungeon of hell for their cowardice. Immediately upon hearing of what had happened, HSM sent forth a battalion to forestall whatever came next in the plan of the Invasion. Some theorists had mistakenly believed that this "Incarnation" (as the awful name has been coined) would meet with instant acclamation. A devil, whose name I will not mention because he has been rehabilitated, had this very stupid idea. He forgot that the Enemy's whole plan involved convincing the half-clods of his union to their miserable state, something birth alone could not do.

Within microseconds of the retreat of the Lost Legion, as it has been called, our troops were flying around Bethlehem to ward off the first ceremony of recognition planned by the Enemy.

CHAPTER TWENTY-THREE:
THE SHEPHERDS

[Another podcast-like transcript, although I am uncertain it is by the same hand as the preceding. –Informant]

The Pretender's first "royal" reception involved some poor shepherds who were lying with their flocks that cold night in Bethlehem. The miserable bunch were sons of one family. A formidable woman of Judah had given birth to twelve sons. Her husband, a very simple man, had some pretensions in terms of religion. He frequented the synagogue on Sabbaths and sometimes chatted with the rabbi, a most disagreeable man for us, but revered by those who joined him in this study of *you-know-what*. [They hate revelation. –ed.]

This father of twelve sons, whose name was Jacob, had—independent of all information and consultation with his wife, Judith—decided that he would be the father of twelve sons, just like his ancestor whose name he bore. At first, he thought that he would name them for the twelve sons of Jacob, but was discouraged in this by the rabbi. "Why don't you name them for the twelve minor prophets?" asked the rabbi.

And so they came, one screaming baby after another: Hosea, Joel, Amos, Obadiah, Jonah, Micah, Nahum, Habakkuk, Zephaniah, Haggai, Zechariah and Malachi. The family was the talk of little Bethlehem. Most of the benighted denizens of that miserable city thought the prodigious family a wonderful thing. That did not change the frightening poverty in which "the shepherd prophets" lived. They lived close to their animals in many senses of the phrase.

To them our enemies made the first announcement of the Invasion. This would be risible if it were not used to such advantage by the Triune Tyranny. [Notice the difference: "Triune" instead of "Trinitarian." - Informant] Obviously the message was: "The first ones to hear the good news were the poor." They chose these peasants from a pious family for a reason. They were bound to respond to the message of the angels. There they were in the cold, cold, cloudless night—and angels appear to them and tell them to see their Master. Of course, they would be stupid enough to hurry over the hills to the cave! I quote here the report submitted in the court martial trial:

Our troops made it as difficult as possible with a strategy aimed at the particular weakness of each of the shepherds. That we were unable to do so should be obvious by now. The shepherds were able to get to Bethlehem and, although we preyed on their fears and weaknesses, they were able to make it to their rendezvous with the Pretender, and that unfortunately has been memorialized *ad nauseam* in the popular culture of the half-clods.

Hosea, by means of our suggestion, thought he heard

the voice of a woman he loved, distant in the cold night. We thought it would distract him off course, because the particular woman we had evoked had rejected him and had chosen a most disreputable man. It was not as if the man were unaffected by our wiles. He was crying bitter, freezing tears, but the angelic voices overpowered us. He ignored even the hunger of his own heart to go to the manger.

His younger brother Joel was of a fastidious character. He detested insects, probably because he had once stirred up a hive of wasps and been stung severely. For him we created a reverie of locusts on that [Here a word was censored, perhaps it was "fateful"—obviously a difficulty for the régime. -Informant] night. Joel saw wave after wave of locusts, beautiful as bomber squadrons sent against civilians come down at him. Each wave the locusts were larger and larger. They started out the size of regular locusts, and then began to appear to be the size of a man's hands, then like chicken hawks, eventually like vultures, growing in the young man's imagination until they had the dimensions of a horse and rider.

Joel could not see beyond the little circle of the locusts. He lost contact with his brothers and shouted but could hear nothing, not even his own voice in the awful buzz of the insects. He began to pray, which was unfortunate for us. We had hoped that fear would choke his prayer and make him unable to concentrate. His guardian angel must have entered his dreamlike state and helped him to sense that the locusts had fallen and made him hear even the crunch of their external coverings breaking under his sandals.

The next eldest, Amos, we made feel as though he were

walking through fire. Even though it was cold, he sweated and his eyes also teared up, but that was because his imagination supplied the smoke. He marched on as though his imagination were not like a wildfire himself. Fields and fields of fire, clouds of smoke, the smell of burnt wool—there wasn't anything we didn't mimic to trick him. Again, he was mesmerized by the Enemy and did not even believe in his own sense knowledge. [Which was not knowledge at all, only the snares of the devil. –ed.]

Probably the smallest of the shepherd brothers was Obadiah—and none of them were very tall. He made up for his short stature by a very bellicose nature. He loved to think of himself as a warrior. So, we presented him armies in the night, marching over the fields toward Bethlehem, dark hordes of armored soldiers, riding all sorts of beasts. We thought the war would distract him, make him forget the news of the child, but, of course, no. The enemy had made him forget war. He only wanted to see the half-clod Babe in the animal's feeding trough.

Since he was a boy, Jonah had heard the despicable story of the prophet swallowed by the whale—excuse me—big fish. He had never seen the ocean, so he had only the vaguest ideas about what it meant to go out to sea in a ship. Without a doubt he had even less understanding of sea creatures, let alone the imaginary beast invented for the story. This lack of experience actually helped us in our temptation of him. First, we began with the sound of waves, roaring waves that should have terrified the peasant boy, but didn't.

Then we had him imagine water, filling up the dales so that the hills appeared only small circles, as if a man were under water and only the crown of his head would show. Jonah was one of those earthlings who sometimes seem to be living on two levels. It was as if he could see himself from some point well above, walking amid the waves along a ridge in the terrain. He could *almost* feel the water lapping over the edge and touching his feet.

Then, the noise of the Leviathan—what would Jonah know from whales? —it was a sea monster he heard, not a specimen of zoology. The roar had him shaking in his cheap sandals. We really thought we had him, at least. He was trembling, and his breathing was short—the half-clods call it hyperventilating. If he had eaten something more substantial than the bread and cheese he had consumed some hours before, he probably would have vomited—his stomach was churning so much. His eyes darted about in his dreamlike state. We saw he was in full-blown panic, something we like to see in the half-clods.

But then, he suddenly calmed down. Our operatives in his case were completely surprised. Apparently, the music of the angels again had worked against us.

The name Nahum refers to a word for comfort in Hebrew and the devil was inspired to make the young man who bore that moniker so "comfortable" that he would not arrive at the stable. Every stone on the path was made to look like a pillow. Pleasant aromas perfumed the air, which was made sticky with humidity as if the boy were walking in a bubble of vapor in the cold night. His eyelids became heavy as soothing music played in his ears with the words, "Rest, Rest, Rest," repeated. He actually lay down on the frozen ground and reclined his head on a stone without feeling any discomfort at all. Unfortunately, his bladder woke him up, stimulated by the cold. When he awakened, the spell snapped and he walked briskly to catch up with his brother Jonah.

Micah was a young man we thought more susceptible. We made the starlit night as black as a cave for him. He could not see his brothers who were only a few feet ahead of him, all walking along in enchanted silence. The silence is what unsettled us. A human being who is silent is almost always trouble for us. They make noises when they interact, and where there is interaction, temptation always finds some means of seeping in. Micah walked in total obscurity with an astonishing confidence. We suspect the Enemy, of course, of guiding his steps.

With Habakkuk, we tried another tactic. We had him imagine bandits moving about in gangs amid the hills. The idea was to make the young man fear that these armed groups of men would steal all the sheep of their miserable family. His heart raced, his tongue clave to his palate, beetles roiled about in his abdomen, his legs felt like they were made of the leather used for whips—all the trite clichés of half-clod emotional reactions—but it was good for nothing. He subdued his fears, he swallowed hard, and he rubbed his stomach and marched on, climbing the hills and dales as if he were a young deer.

Zephaniah was one of those intense types that give us such trouble. Obsessed by what is beyond their grasp, they practically forget they live on earth. Everyone who knew him said that the boy should have been a priest. Of course, he was of the wrong stock, but he could have been a rabbi. He was never as happy as he was when his father let him accompany him to synagogue on Saturdays. His education was poor, but he read the different scrolls with a sense of awe with which it is difficult to fight.

The devils assigned to him tried to make him doubt the

announcement of the birth. Why would the angels come to them, poor shepherds, and not to the leaders of the people? With his simple piety, Zephaniah expected that the announcement would be better made in the Temple of Jerusalem, to which he had accompanied his father two times.

Our agents made Zephaniah consider the possibility that the angels who had proclaimed the birth of the Messiah were actually devils trying to trick the poor shepherds into wandering around at night, leaving the sheep unprotected. Zephaniah paused to think about that possibility, because he had a scrupulous tendency. We could see him almost accept the idea that he was in the midst of a great deception, a false prophecy that presaged the wrath of God. Then the Enemy beat us back. The window of opportunity for sin closed and Zephaniah marched forward, if anything more optimistic than he had been. We had not used sensate temptations, and so to punish the boy for his resistance we made him stub his toe. Even that failed to get a reaction from him, or rather, he was so ecstatic about "seeing" the angels that he did not get bothered by the pain. The next day he hobbled about, but that night he kept the same pace as his fast-moving brothers.

With Zechariah, there was another strategy. An agent appeared to him as an angel, something quite dangerous to do considering the presence of the enemy troops. Then four horsemen came riding over to the boy. He asked the angel who they were, and our agent said that these horsemen had been "sent" to take him where he wanted to go. The idea was to have him try to mount the imaginary beast and fall into the ravine, where we calculated that he would break his neck. He got close to the imaginary horseman, even touching the imaginary bridle. Just as he was about to swing his leg up to the beast on the edge of a canyon where a creek flowed at the bottom, his brother Hosea saw him and said, "Are you falling asleep again?" Apparently, the boy was a somnambulist and the brothers had caught him several times in precarious circumstances.

Malachi was the youngest brother. In fact, his elders did not want to bring him along, something we used to make him walk apart from them. Then we had fire appear to him, and the smell of incense in the air. "Why go on?" voices said to him. "Your brothers hate you. Stay here." He was on the brink of tears, and we might have delayed him, but at the last minute his brother Zephaniah stumbled upon him and the two walked together to the cave.

CHAPTER TWENTY-FOUR: THE ARRIVAL OF THE SHEPHERDS

When they came to the stable, it was like seeing one of those half-clod movies in slow motion. [So, they do go to the cinema. –ed.] They were completely silent, and their movements seemed coordinated somehow. While it would not seem possible that half-clod senses could perceive their entrance, Miriam and Joseph looked up quite unafraid as they saw the young men coming.

The faces of the shepherds showed how enraptured they were with the scene. Who knows what tricks the Enemy played to make the young half-clods feel instantly the presence of Number Two. They were enthralled, totally transported to another state of feeling, one they had never sensed before. Their eyes glistened with tears, their hearts melted within them like a candle thrown into a fire—all the shabby tricks of their nature that we usually turn to our advantage were present but working, instead, for the Other Side.

Quickly they knelt down to pray. And it was a prayer so intense, sincere and personal, that our company had to withdraw. It was an unfortunate, awful, terrible little skirmish. We could do nothing to stop it and the shepherds almost danced in slow motion when they came up to give obeisance to the Pretender. It was typical that the Pretender be worshipped first by the great unwashed, so to speak, and we resented the ploy, but could do nothing.

The ridiculous strategy of lowering the divinity to the level of the half-clods had success with these poor shepherds because they had no sophistication. They didn't seem to think it incongruous that the glory they sensed in the child was juxtaposed with the wretchedness of the stable. For them it did not seem illogical that they would kneel to three people as poor as themselves in the cold of a night when they would have been better off building a fire and sitting around it comfortably. They had no sense of the monstrous disproportion involved in worshipping their God swaddled in a feeding trough in a cave with animals around. They were so stupid that we could not get them to reject what they felt in their hearts.

There was such peace around the little hill on which the cave stood that we ended up falling back to positions quite a distance away. Of course, we could see how each of the shepherds came close to the manger and how they variously expressed their reverence. Most kissed the foot of the Pretender, a sight so disgusting to us in its simplicity that some devils in the company howled with pain and rage. Malachi, the youngest, touched the face of the baby in the manger with his forefinger, caressing him gently.

He claimed that the baby smiled at him. We believe that it is possible that some combination of facial muscle movement approximating the half-clod reaction of contentment contorted the infant's face for a few seconds. Hosea, who stood watching his brother, cleared his throat, but then did nothing. From that moment on, Malachi was lost to us. He never forgot the tenderness and awe of that moment, and he died quite young for a half-clod, in disgusting innocence.

From this skirmish came the hymn of the so-called loyalist angels, whom we call more appropriately the cowardly ones. It is worth putting the lines down here just as an example of how pathetic the angelic submission to the Enemy has become. The angels, spiritual beings, worship a half-clod. There is no getting around the infamy. A superior being in adoration of one that is at least half inferior.

Angels, descend, the Babe calls to us silently
Archangels, behold our Maker made man
Principalities, the true Prince sleeps in a manger
Virtues, admire the wondrous strength given to his father and mother
Powers, on your guard, for evil lurks around them
Dominations, acclaim the Lord born in a stable
Ye Thrones, give glory to Him who exchanged heaven for earth
Cherubim, keep watch o'er Divine Truth Incarnate
Seraphim, burn and give the Child light and warmth
Nine choirs of Angels are nine choirs of praise
We adore Him, we adore Him, we adore Him
Creator-creature

[No poetry in translation really works. You can capture a few images, but it is a hopeless task to convey the music of even human poetry written in a language not our own. And the angels sing this! –Informant]

A most disgusting doggerel, unworthy of our nature. Utter shamelessness.

CHAPTER TWENTY-FIVE:
THE MAGI

The second part of the Plan had to do with the Magi. I will not retell the whole story of the Magi here. Their personal profiles, strengths and weaknesses, how they were called, what it took for them to decide to join forces, the way in which their primitive religion was used by the Enemy as a tool for the recognition of the Pretender, the vagaries of their journey through the various monarchies and city-states of the time—all of these can be found with more detail in the relevant archives. After a brief sketch, we will take up the story when the Magi arrived in Jerusalem, and give only the briefest of biographies.

[Gap here in the file: censorship or missing citation of another document? –ed.]

A little background of the three unlikely dupes of the TT. I shall begin with that Nubian dreamer known to legend as Casper. Some of the clodlings think the "black" wise man was named Balthazar, but that is only one of the traditions, perhaps based on the more exotic quality of the name. This Casper was the son of a tribal leader, and, in fact, there is evidence that his peculiar chemical makeup, the famous "DNA" half-clods are always chirping about, contains some traces of the historic men who left Nubia to conquer Egypt. They became the black Pharaohs, but of course left some people behind in the home country.

Among them were the ancestors of this miserable Casper, so half-clod tradition is not wrong in assigning him "royal" degree. However, he was born in more than modest circumstances. His stepfather (his mother had been a widow and herself died young) sold him into slavery. The merchant of humans took him to a market in Memphis, the ancient capital of Egypt. Casper was considered a fine specimen of human chattel and was purchased by some Jewish priests who worked in the strange heretical temple of Onias, some twenty miles from Memphis.

Onias, as some will remember, was a Yahwist who did not believe that only the Temple in Jerusalem was an adequate place to worship their God. He was exiled during the troubles of the Maccabean era in Judea and, by winning favor with one of those endlessly boring number of Ptolemys, was granted land for a "temple." There Jews who did not wish to travel to Jerusalem could offer sacrifices.

The place had its utility for us. It effectively separated a community of Jewish Egyptians from the living tradition of their ancestors while pretending to do just the opposite. It is the ancient strategy of HSM to make people believe their religious experience is superior to their own tradition. "Divide and rule." The temple of Onias was "just as good" as Jerusalem, it was argued. The sacrifices were scrupulously similar, perhaps even better because not so tainted by politics. It was just the way that the authoritative tradition that had been adjusted to contemporary standards and conveniences. Jews were living in Egypt: why couldn't they have a place of worship there, also? The atomizing gambit has worked for us many different times. Unfortunately, the whole game collapsed, but it was a useful experiment.

So, this Nubian "prince" lived for a while in a Jewish environment. Casper was thus exposed to Jewish thought and religious practice. First he learned Greek and then some Hebrew. Seeing that he was a clever boy, his master taught him how to read Hebrew and would have had him circumcised, but had been beaten to the trick. [Most likely, his circumcision had been tribal, adolescent and very painful, a puberty ritual custom. Did the Nubians give it to the Egyptians? The Jews, after all, had picked up the custom from the Egyptians. -Informant] Casper learned a great deal of history and—sad to say—theology from his master. However, the devils in charge of his area put the master to the test. The man who bought Casper fought with the so-called high priest, and was banished from the Temple. That meant that there was no further participation in the funds from the treasury of the Temple and he had to make do with his savings. He invested in an "opportunity" that did work out so well. As a result, he had to sell Casper.

That is where a strange coincidence occurred that of course was nothing of the kind. Our enemy had skillfully prepared an expedition for another of the famous "magoi" [Sometimes they use the Greek and at other times the Latin, diabolical caprices? -Informant] who was called Balthazar that included a visit to Alexandria. He was the most famous of the three and in a way the leader. Why was this magus in Egypt? Egypt, of course, had formerly been a Persian possession. Alexander, called "the Great" by the half-clod yahoos, had wrested it out of Persian dominion and had caused its incomplete "Hellenization." But the Persians did not forget their former glory, and were still interested in Egypt.

The great Alexander had built the capital for the Greeks who ruled Egypt and modestly named it after himself. Memphis remained the sort of "Vatican" [ha ha ha –ed.] of Egyptian religion, but the Greek rulers were living in Alexandria, along with many other people, including a huge concentration of the Chosen People. The city founded by the megalomaniac was a center of learning and commerce. That is where Casper was taken by his master, the ex-priest down on his heels. Casper was in his twenties, not prepared for physical work but educated, with skills in language and writing that were more marketable in Alexandria. Memphis to Alexandria was a dramatic change for the man.

Why a magus would visit a slave market in Egypt is something even we cannot completely ascertain. Perhaps he wanted some kind of company that would open new perspectives to him. Anyway, the Persian found himself in the Alexandrian slave market, one of our more exotic watering holes. [An approximate metaphor for saying the devils enjoyed hanging around such places. –Informant] Perhaps the dealer had sensed in Balthazar an unusual person—some half-clods have kind of an intuition of such things sometimes; they usually are called entrepreneurs—and had decided to get a lot of money for him. (This idea had been given him by a devil who was totally ignorant of the Enemy's plans for Balthazar and Casper. Nevertheless, the devil was given duty with condemned souls for a millennium because some standards must be kept.)

Balthazar was a Magus of great wealth. Now I must explain who the Magi were and why we thought they would help us at first. We always appreciate the value of castes. With castes, there is always a great deal of room for us to play in. There is, as a given, pride in the caste, a penchant for exclusion, a sense of superiority over others, a dislike if not disdain of mixing with those not alike. Interests, not principles are what matter with castes. Self-interest, of course, is for us the compass of human misconduct. It can little abide the truth. That is why castes live on deception. Then there are the intrigues within the caste, the internecine struggles, the betrayals, and all the delicious back-and-forth of human infidelity and betrayal.

The Magi (in the institutional form) were a caste that had originated as the priesthood among the Medes. When Cyrus and the Persians conquered Babylon, these people somehow managed to retain power and this in the teeth of Cyrus' real antipathy for them. They survived even a failed *coup d'état* against the Persians and when these last were destroyed by Alexander and the Hellenic forces, the Magi regrouped with the Parthians. These were members of a Persian tribe more brutal than others and this helped their ascent to power. The Parthians were so ferocious, even the Roman legions could not conquer them. They made the Euphrates the boundary between the two "empires." Within the Parthian government, the Magi had a kind of legislature—their own kind of organization, independent of the tribal leaders. They were clever men and they knew it and even how to hide it at times behind a sort of abstract technical "innocence."

The Magi studied the stars so much, it was considered that they knew more than others about the future. This is the ironic thing about human ignorance. The stars reveal the past of the physical universe, but the half-clod would like to think they reveal the future—their personal future. Things like: "are they going to win money? or find a boyfriend?" they hope to read from the gaseous fires of other suns. They are absolutely helpless when they mass together because whatever idea is more contradictory to the truth appeals to them more. If there were not so much interference from some a certain quarter, they would be little work for us with these humans.

The Parthians were superstitious, which helped the Magi considerably. The Parthian nobles would run to the astronomers with dreams that were the result of too many supper parties too late at night, with too much libation. A Magus would study the case with a seriousness that compelled attention. And then pronounce ambiguities with a dignified air.

Balthazar's family tree included some Parthian princesses, among them one who was a distant cousin of the reigning monarch. It could thus be said that he had royal blood in his veins. Within the order of the Magi, Balthazar was treated with special favor and had unique privileges. He was not a bad student, and he had been given classes by the greatest Magi astronomers. He was a restless sort, however, and was always looking for something more. Unfortunately, our agents were unable to exploit this trait. Instead, it was exploited by our Enemy. He did this when he introduced among the Magi a certain Tibetan-Chinese-Indo-Parthian named Melchior.

Half-clods are always following trade routes, criss-crossing the globe to meet each other and find some novelties to amuse their weak intelligences. The whole world is a kind of marketplace for them, and their *wanderlust* has them roaming about. Obviously, this is usually to our advantage, but sometimes the Enemy insinuates Himself, as in this case. You can all have reference to the histories that delineate the bloodlines of ancient empires. I will summarize in this way: a half-Tibetan, half-Chinese married a full Tibetan whose daughter married an Indo-Parthian and then they travelled west to Parthia proper.

The child of their union was Melchior. He was given an education by the Magi, no doubt because his father had somehow traded bales of silk into rubies in his odyssey and was that strange sort of case of a fabulously wealthy man who hid his wealth from all but a few people. These last included the Magi, who were masters of intrigue (and finance), besides being accomplished astronomers. Of course, the astronomers were not usually the administrators of the order, nor the intriguers. They were a special breed of half-clods that practically worshipped the material universe and its designs; something we feel is a bit disgusting, of course. Melchior was taken up by the astronomers and proved a wonderful student. His exotic extraction appealed to the universalist strain in Magian ideology and so did his Buddhist background.

He grew old and became a leader in a very special subset of Magi and he developed all sorts of strange ideas. Among them was that he could read in the heavens the advent of a world-savior even greater than Gautama Buddha and Zoroaster. Because of his unique perspective, he was consulted by many Parthian nobles, even about their absurd dreams and petty ambitions. He heard all with an inscrutable air and this increased his reputation as a wise man. Even though the Magian hierarchy considered him a heretic—he never assisted at their fire worship, for instance—he was untouchable because of his popularity with certain very influential people.

He had not succeeded in developing a school, however, and had no disciples before Balthazar became interested in him. Evidence suggests that he sent Balthazar out on the expedition because he hoped that the younger man might be his ticket to greater influence among the Magi. Through the younger man, the older one wanted to guide the assembly of the Magi.

As soon as Balthazar came back from Alexandria, he presented Caspar to Melchior. Why our guards seemed to ignore all this movement is still a puzzle to us. The Enemy had subtly thrown us off the chase. The chemistry between the three was extraordinary. Soon they had cooked up a universalist theory of a "Savior" whose star they would follow to a sort of "epiphany" of recognition (I use the word without succumbing to the religious propaganda that has tarnished it).

They were not three "kings" but in some respects were royal. They represented a threat to us that was hard to discern. If we had been able to identify the uses the Enemy would make of these three peculiar Magi, we might have been able to succeed in interrupting the Invasion at a point previous to the denouement that we all know and detest.

When Balthazar bought the young Judaized Nubian, the Enemy had assembled a team. The bloodlines of the three men embraced the globe. This was part of the sneakiness behind the whole thing. They also represented three different ages: Melchior was an old man; Balthazar was middle-aged; Caspar was young. Melchior had roots in the merchant class, although one ancestress was the sister of a Lama. Balthazar was from the aristocratic priestly caste. Caspar the Nubian was a slave and a prince at the same time. The old man had Buddhist connections, the young man Jewish, the middle-aged one the mix of Mede and Persian religions. This is how our Enemy works. Every detail is planned out. We must learn to combat the Trinitarian Tyranny with our own details. All Hail His Satanic Majesty! Eternal Dominance! We Stopped the Invasion! [It seems these cheers might be interpolations of an editor nervous about a devil giving God his due. – Informant]

The coincidence that was not a coincidence was that all our High Command's attention was on the Palestinian theater while the three Magi were staring at the skies waiting for their sign. We still do not know what they saw. Some have thought that there was a comet or a supernova, but the whole star story could be an example of how the half-clods compress all sorts of data into smooth little vignettes. What if Melchior claimed that some configuration gave proof of the Messiah's birth and then Caspar connected that to the Jews and Balthazar suggested a visit to that country? The same story, but not as dramatic as a star that only the Magi could see in the autumn skies of Mesopotamia. The more complicated narrative is more difficult and less poetic. It is also not easy to be retold.

Obviously, we have a great deal of intelligence data about Scripture scholars. Many of them have been very well guarded by us and we have promoted them academically. (This has been helped by their very obvious pride—arrogance is a fairly common trait). We have used

Scripture scholarship to our own purposes because half-clods love sophistication more than wisdom. They like to think they see through things that others accept. This idea of a special "gnosis" has served us wonderfully.

The Gnostic Strategy failed as a specific campaign against Christianity, but little currents of Gnosticism have served us well through the centuries. Just think about how scholars have helped us with the story of the Magi, getting lost in all sorts of historical speculation and missing the great meaning that the Enemy wanted to convey: a universal event that would overturn our government of the world, or rather, attempt to do so.

CHAPTER TWENTY-SIX:
OUR RESPONSE TO THE MAGI THREAT: THE JERUSALEM SEQUENCE

As we have seen earlier, we considered Herod's court as one of our playgrounds. The fact that the Magi were led to that very court caught us off guard. The High Command could not believe that the Enemy had shown His hand (another half-clod saying, referring to a delightful game played with colored cardboard that has helped to lose some souls) by allowing the Persian priests to stumble into our precincts.

Later we learned that the whole affair was an elaborate decoy operation, which enabled the Pretender and his "parents" to escape the Palestine Theater. The Enemy wanted us to jump to conclusions. Herod's capriciousness, which we had used so frequently for our own ends, was a problem in these new circumstances, as we will show.

But first there is a point to be made about their arrival. The Magi were noticed as soon as they crossed the Euphrates, the border between the Parthian lands and the Roman Empire. The governor in Syria immediately knew that the three were going to Jerusalem and Herod was advised. Since the Romans knew that Herod would always do his best for them, they took a hands-off attitude towards the case. It was not even reported to the Emperor as yet, because it was considered a diplomatic feeler, and more facts had to be known before involving the imperial bureaucracy.

The Magi made a stately progress. The commoner half-clods were most impressed with the retinue that accompanied these three oddballs and were calling them "kings." The Magi were apparently in no rush to get to the birth of the Pretender. Please note the "apparently" used here. Their visit would coincide with several circumstances that were advantageous for the kind of subversive activity implied in the Invasion. We were caught off guard by the strange, indirect way the Enemy was acting.

Herod's court was in its *Ragnarokian* finale, its own nihilistic *Gotterdammerung*-like apotheosis. [I told you the devil likes to use big words and convoluted imagery and these are from Norse mythology, and Wagner! –ed.] Three years earlier, the king had killed his two sons by his Hasmonean wife Mariamne, Aristobulus and Alexander. This had been at the instigation of his oldest son, Antipater, one of our protégés, and Salome, Herod's sweet sister. Although Antipater was declared heir to the throne briefly, his father's ideas soon changed. Herod himself, probably in a drunken stupor, wondered why he had killed his two Hasmonean sons, after allowing them to live so many years after he put their mother to death. He blamed Antipater for the deed. His first punishment was to change his will. For Antipater, the change of heir-apparent was only a reprieve of a more drastic punishment; his head would bounce along afterward.

Because he was changing his will, Herod called his descendants to Jerusalem. This would have fateful consequences with regard to the Invasion because the group would be so involved in intrigues that there was an inadequate response made to the Magi and their revelations.

Our agents still had hope for Antipater. We thought that he would be best for Israel because he was an Idumean. It was our policy at the time to promote whatever would be disadvantageous to the Jewish religion. The Hasmoneans were regarded favorably by a portion of the Jewish people. They were descendants of the Maccabees and were religiously orthodox. Herod, who had married a Hasmonean princess, feigned religious orthodoxy, but at the same time built pagan temples and had sacrifices offered for his intentions by pagan priests. He really had quite a modern spirit and it is unfortunate that his reputation is so miserable, all because of what happened in his clean-up operation in Bethlehem. Alas, he was born too soon and could not live in an age of religious tolerance [Diabolic Sanskrit for the New Age spirituality. –Informant] when the massacre of the innocents is practically state policy in some places.

So, Herod's palace was filled with Herod's sons by all his various wives. It was a wonderful environment: they all hated each other. I shall list them all: Antipater was the son of the first wife, Doris. Herod had set her aside in order to solidify his claims to the throne by marrying his first Mariamne (the delightful thing about Herod is that he insisted on confusing people so much with multiple sons that were namesakes, duplicate wives with the same name, etc., he was quite a genius at obfuscation).

Next came Herod Phillip, son of the "other" Mariamne (both were daughters of high priests, so don't worry).

Herod Philip, aka Herod II, was briefly named heir to the throne by his monstrous father. However, the "great" Herod changed his mind and sent him to live in Rome as a kind of ambassador-spy. He is most famous for allowing his younger half-brother, Herod Antipas, to carry off his wife Herodias, a circumstance that is important in the history of the Invasion because of John the Baptist (but that is outside the scope of this lecture). Herodias—here we have an example of the incestuous ingenuity of these Herodians—was also a granddaughter of Herod the So-called Great. She was the daughter of the dead Alexander, the son of the first (and murdered) Mariamme. This family was brilliant in infamy and deserves its special place in Hell.

Herod's fourth wife was Malthace, a Samaritan, and she bore him two sons, Archelaus and Herod Antipas. The latter would get tangled with his niece Herodias. Then, in a lustful drunken binge he helped us eliminate the Baptizer because of a dance of his grand-niece and quasi adopted daughter Salome. That spiteful little girl was named for her great-great aunt Salome, who was the sister of Herod "the Great" who had engineered the destruction of her sister-in-law, the first Mariamne, as well as Herod's and her own blood brother (yes, Old Boy Herod was also a fratricide, killing a brother at the instigation of their common sister, which really beats Cain and Abel, if you think about it).

The son of Herod's fifth wife, Cleopatra of Jerusalem, was also present. His name was simply Philip, to distinguish him from his half-brother Herod Philip, whose daughter Salome (by the delightful Herodias) he married. He was given a territory as tetrarch and married Salome, the dancing little dervish, but the couple had no children. Not until the advent of television reality shows and the family K. did we have so much satisfaction working with a family. If you can't wrap your angelic intelligences around that, pity the poor half-clods. You must know I am joking, of course, a dirty joke, if you will, because pity is a loathsome thing. [These asides seem to indicate either interpolation or another author than most of the above file. –ed.]

Everyone knew that Herod was trying to decide who should be king "*après lui.*" [There he goes again with the French, meaning "after him," probably a devilish allusion to "*après moi, le deluge*" of Louis XIV. –ed.] And then the Magi showed up, ruining our game. It was the adjustment of our plans that had to do with the clever way the Magi could come and insinuate the presence of the Messiah but not give anything away. If Herod had not been so sick, perhaps he would have responded better to our suggestions. And, of course, making Antipater, his disaffected son, the chosen promotor of our ideas was an unfortunate miscalculation.

As was said previously, our agents were not exactly on top of the Enemy's Magi initiative. You have seen all that was going on in the Palestinian Theater and can understand why some speculation by a marginal group in a pagan priestly caste could escape thorough-going notice in those halcyon pre-Invasion days.

A word about the "star." The stellar coordinates were not changed for this purpose. Rather, and that has been a well-kept secret from half-clods, the Magi astronomers' interpretation of the constellations led them to believe that they were headed to where the Messiah would be born. [Sic, this seems redundant, as per above, but could show that another author's work is included. –ed.] Their destination was always Palestine; it is really too much to believe they didn't know where they were headed from the start. The idea of following a star moving across the heavens, as reported in the Enemy's propaganda, is a symbolic summary of events that is easy for half-clods to grasp and communicate one small mind to another. Of course, there are literalists, for which we should be grateful, since they cause a perpetual *cognitive dissonance* in religious circles. [The devils apparently love catch-phrases, too. –ed.]

So, of course, the "star" would lead the Magi to Jerusalem. The Jewish Messiah would be the World Savior, according to the theory the three astronomers had supposedly cooked up by themselves and Jerusalem was the political and religious capital of the Jewish kingdom. The trouble was that troops had been pulled out of Jerusalem because of what was happening in Bethlehem. That explains why there was an unfortunate delay in actions taken, of which more later.

Caspar, Melchior and Balthazar had apprised the Magi Council that they were going on an expedition that might take them as far as Egypt. The Council, which was more interested in the Parthian candidates for succession to the throne, had no objections to their going. This was another key victory for the Enemy's strategy. The fact that the Council knew about the journey of the Magi made it, in the eyes of Herod and his court, a semi-official mission. Actually, they would not have bothered about the "semi." The result was that Herod felt compelled to be very careful in his dealings with the three men, with the obvious disadvantages for us.

The caravan arrived at court and caused an extraordinary amount of curiosity. As soon as the Magi were recognized, a *frisson* ran up and down the spine of the city. [Why do the devils love this French word so much? –ed.] What were the Parthians up to? Herod's court was about to explode in violence. Very soon after this, he would change his plans for the succession and murder his firstborn son. The relationship between the two events should be obvious, but it is not to the half-clods, whom we have distracted for at least the last four hundred years saying that the Magi never existed.

Herod was at a meeting with his Greek advisor Dionysius, famous for being an official "philosopher" of the court, when the news was brought that the Magi had arrived. Their lodgings were already prepared, with slaves in attendance who could understand the Persian tongue in order to eavesdrop.

"Please bring them to me and tell them that I insist they be my guests."

When the Magi were brought in and Herod saw them in the smaller throne room, everyone wondered what was going to happen. Of course, many thought the Magi were going to bring some kind of impossible demand from the Parthians despots. It was expected that an ultimatum would be followed by a war. The Roman spies had thought that war was not a possibility given the uncertainty about the Parthian succession. At least some people in the Syrian governor's court thought the Magi were representing a candidate for the Parthian throne who wanted to play the diplomatic card to get Herod's—and hence, Rome's—support.

Herod was quite gracious to his visitors, as he was

with most people outside of his family and the Jewish priesthood. How honored he was that the Magi had come. He had to insist, of course, that they stay at the palace, instead of with the Persian merchant who had offered them hospitality. (Of course, there were some Persians in trade in Jerusalem, spies mostly.)

"I have already prepared your lodgings," Herod said, brushing away their protests.

"We have just arrived; how could you have places prepared for us?" asked Melchior.

Herod smiled. "Since you crossed the Euphrates, you have been under surveillance. I was sure you were bound for our holy city."

Of course, the Magi knew this, but they were taken off guard by the old fox's candor. It is a universal rule in half-clod behavior that wicked people can trick others by saying the truth. Herod proceeded to confess his admiration for the Magi. He was fascinated by all that was foreign, a true "philosopher-king" in that aspect. The old bugger was curious.

The Magi saw that Herod was genuinely interested in learning something new. Balthazar, especially, was quite taken with the king. Perhaps the idiot recognized a kindred spirit through the distortions of a perverse murderer. It is ironic that saints always see something in the worst of criminals that makes them sympathetic to sinners. The opposite is not true, generally, for which we thank [missing –Informant].

The first tactics with the Magi were inexpedient. We thought we could make the Magi reject the whole idea of a Universal Savior coming out of Israel. The devils kept insinuating two points: 1. Jews know less than the

Persians; and 2. assigning of universal meaning to the Jewish Messiah was to allow the particularity of a minority nation, only a small part of the Persian province of Yehud for centuries, to achieve cosmic religious dimensions. With these particular thoughts went some doubts about the stargazing of the old monsters who had taught them and whether the calculations they used had been accurate. The journey was difficult, travelling as they did with so many servants across various political lines, and we introduced the feeling that it all might end up being an exercise in futility. They might as well have a good time and stay in Jerusalem.

This approach was misconceived because the three star-struck numbskulls had already worked through these temptations. There was a certain air of *déjà vu* about them. Old temptations work when the subject is feeling weak or lonely or frustrated or angry. These three were having the time of their miserable little lives. They were riding the crest of a wave, as the half-clods say. They were not about to doubt themselves.

The next strategy was to get Herod to kill the Magi. This also was not a workable plan, because the crafty old king did not want a war with the Parthians. It did not really matter, however, because the person we were counting on to do the assassination was Antipater, Herod's eldest and most hateful son.

CHAPTER TWENTY-SEVEN: CASPAR AND ANTIPATER

Antipater maneuvered to see the Magi on his own, away from his father. This should have been easy, but Herod was much taken by the three dolts and hardly let them out of his sight. His son was also very interested in the prophecy of the Magi and wanted very much to know about the birth of the Pretender. This was not because he knew who the Pretender might be, but because he was obsessed with the succession. He had just been demoted from heir apparent, but he still had hopes. He didn't know that shortly after the visit of the Magi, his father would have him put to death and then die himself. Exit: Antipater and "just in time" was how one of my sources put it. He was wrong.

I will quote here from the memoirs of Casper, which were lost to the half-clods, but indicate the kind of sneakiness that was engaged in by the Pretender and his forces.

Herod was a most crafty and subtle person. His kingdom and his history had demonstrated the value of suspicion as a policy of state. He doubted and despised everyone around him, even his own children, not to mention his wives.

He received us with an artificiality that had us quite amazed. His propensity for lying was astonishing even in the circles we moved in. My colleagues (aka old partners in crime according to our enemies) Balthazar and Melchior said that they had never met a man for whom dishonesty appeared so natural. "He was one who probably could lie to his mother while still a babe in her arms," said Melchior. No one could have been smoother showing interest in our story of the Universal King. Only Balthazar appeared to be taken in by him (at first, of course).

The old king was in a paranoid state. He knew he had to die soon but somehow was hoping that an elixir would be found that would gain him more time. "You probably have heard of the fountain whose water regenerates an old man and makes him young again," he said to us, "I do not believe in it."

Of course, we had not heard of it and he did believe in it. He just hoped that we could tell him how to get there. He knew that his time was very short. You could see the struggle in his face. His concern was how to manage the succession so that it would be just an extension of himself. He believed that he would be remembered as a great King. How pathetic that seems, considering that one of his last royal acts was the murder of babies. Although he took great care to make us think of him as a very rare ruler, humble and religious, I could hear that a wolf's heart beat under the rich damask cloth he wore. His eyes were constantly reading us, as if he were an actor anxious to know how his audience was taking his performance.

I received a visit from Antipater the morning after our interview with his father. His unfortunate first impression *was that I was only a servant of the other Magi. That was thanks to my dark skin, I suppose, but he was soon disabused. I told him that he could speak to me with confidence, that we three were completely at one and to speak to one of us was the same as speaking to all of us, only easier and less "public." He liked that note of discretion.*

He was surprised that I spoke Aramaic, although I did not speak it so well, it being the sixth tongue that I have learned. He seemed to prefer Aramaic to Greek. "My father's spies all speak Greek. Aramaic they know less," he said with an air of mystery, as if he were about to tell me some great secret.

He really didn't want to give anything away. In that he showed he was well-schooled by the demons who had him in their control. (The nerve of the little astrologer, accusing us of having taught Antipater. The trouble was that he did not learn enough from us, the loser!) *Antipater was afraid, with good reason, as things turned out, that his father's murderous caprices would eventually point his way, too. Since he had had much to do with his father's family murders, he knew that old King Herod would stop at nothing.*

"This child—he is born already?"

"Apparently so," I answered the prince.

He took the news like a knife wound to the stomach. Antipater had the dark good looks of an Arabian prince, with a thick black beard framing his face. The black color of his eyes was blacker than my own and combined with his thick eyebrows gave off a sense of power just barely under control.

"Well, there is nothing left for us to do but celebrate,

and invite the prodigy to the palace."

He said this in a still, small voice and it seemed like he himself were listening to his own words with wonder. I thought perhaps he had said what he was thinking I wanted to hear, without really wanting to say it. Or perhaps a devil was prompting him. (He puts out this last as if it is an afterthought. How he would know this is the subject of controversy. Some say that half-clods sometimes have access to hidden knowledge—not communicated immediately by sensory experience—but it is more likely that Caspar was enlightened by *You Know Who*). [The Holy Spirit? –ed.]

Antipater invited us to a dinner in his part of the palace. Melchior immediately suspected a plot. He asked whether we should bring servants to test the food. Balthazar was shocked, as I was. Would we put our servants in danger that way? In the end, I was sent by myself. I said that we could not participate that evening because we were fasting due to an astrological phenomenon—the alignment of the planets, and so forth. Antipater was the least "Greek" of Herod's family. He probably thought that there might be something to the excuse we used, because he accepted the excuse without argument, but was disappointed and confused.

Later Melchior said that perhaps we should have risked the supper. "The demons that make Antipater dance are probably not sure what to do next. Some of them might be for poisoning us, but others probably want to know where the child is and hope we will lead Antipater to him. (Ludicrous! As if we didn't know where the Child was! Besides, our agents had already ruled out the poisoning plot before the Nubian Magi arrived. In fact, the slave who had been charged to make the poisoned victuals had been forced to eat them himself. Because he had thoughtfully imbibed an antidote beforehand, he had only suffered a severe sickness, but did not die.)

Antipater offered to accompany me out to the patio where the walkway to our quarters was. I feared at first that he would stab me in the shadows of the colonnade. Then I wondered if he would take me all the way back to the quarters and find the others eating Persian food, the smell of which would have been unmistakable for him.

Fortunately, he paused near a fountain. I could barely see his face because of the clouded sky.

"My father only feigns interest in the child," he said. "If he can get close to the little one, he will have him killed. I would suggest that you allow some of my servants to accompany you. We can hide the child from my father."

At that moment, I received the first and last vision of my life. It was as if I were transported in time and from one place to another. I was in the courtyard, but suddenly the palace disappeared from view. I smelled burning houses; in my mouth I tasted ashes. I heard hysterical screams of women and vicious shouting of soldiers and the thump of horses. There were piercing cries of children, each one interrupted suddenly. My eyes could not believe what I was seeing, soldiers murdering babies like butchers. I trembled in the chill of the vision, so much so that Antipater turned and looked at me with great attention. His reaction made me wonder whether he saw what I had been seeing, but apparently he did not.

"I find it hard to believe this of your father. What you say is quite perturbing," I said. My voice cracked as I said this; my heart was still beating fast and hard from the

vision. I was glad for the sudden inspiration. He might have been only testing me. Even though we were next to the fountain, and the splash of the water masked our conversation from others who could have been hiding in the courtyard, I had to be cautious.

"I say it with regret, of course," answered Antipater. My father does not love me, but I have loved him. He is a dying man, that is obvious to all who know him, but sometimes I think that he will kill me before he dies."

It was a cool night. I half expected ice to form in the fountain. There were some stoves set up in the portico to warm the space between the lower and the upper palace, but they did nothing for us standing next to the fountain. I daresay Antipater did not feel the cold while he spoke. There were beads of sweat on his forehead. He was so intent on plotting against his own father. Balthazar said afterwards, when I had told him the whole story, that perhaps Antipater was hoping a Parthian alliance would put him on the throne. Evidently, he was obsessed with his father's crown. I am sure he would have given his soul to the devil to win it. (Metaphysical speculations of a Magi. If he only knew! He gave his soul and did not get the crown!)

When I left Antipater, he stared after me a long time. I turned only once, but I felt his eyes upon me. He was consumed with the task of finding out where the child was. Balthazar said that no doubt Antipater was the one who told his father to let us go alone and then return. It was the kind of cleverness King Herod loved: to appear to trust but to achieve his aim anyway. I doubt, however, that father and son had even talked about the issue. When the two were together, there was an almost palpable disgust in the air. I was certain Herod hated his son.

We were to go alone, finally, something we had not even worried about, which shows some of our naiveté. It takes either innocence or stupidity to tell a king that you are seeking his heir with that heir being unknown to him. Herod was smothering us with attention, but he was quite anxious we be on our way. It is as if he had had a premonition of the frustration of his plot. (Really this Casper has a lot of hubris for a half-clod.) But first there was the great show of consultation. King Herod invited a great group of learned men to consult about where the Messiah would be born. He introduced us as "wise men from the East" who wanted to know about the expected Savior of the Jews. The rabbis spent hours debating whether the child could be born in the Diaspora, in Jerusalem or in Bethlehem. One session took six hours and ended up in a cacophony of controversy. The rabbis really knew how to fight, with much scholarly throat-clearing but daggers under their breath.

At last, the King was told that Bethlehem would be the place. He was masterfully disingenuous with us. Would we go and verify the child's whereabouts? And then come back to tell him, so that he could worship the newborn king also. I was looking at Antipater when we were hearing this liar tell us how much he wanted to pay homage to the child who would forever make his name a byword for evil. His face indicated that he was in favor of his father's policy, but was nevertheless afraid.

CHAPTER TWENTY-EIGHT:
SALOME AND BALTHAZAR

All half-clod memoirs are a tissue of lies and half-remembered things. Most of the time, they cannot help themselves: that is their nature. But we had agents there and can say what really happened. The shamelessness of the Magi mission to Jerusalem was revealed in the way the three men played up to one of the real power players at the court: Salome, the sister of King Herod.

As is usual with the Herodian story, there could be confusion if we were to identify this Salome with the dancer who inflamed the pride of Herod the Little, as we called him familiarly, and induced him to put to death the holy prophet John the Baptist. Like the Herods, the Salomes are all related to each other also, but in this case the Salome who was the power in the court of King Herod the Great was the king's sister Salome, the great-great aunt of Salome whom we used to such a good effect to terminate the dread "ministry" of John the Baptist. If we angels sometimes are not clear about all these personages with similar names, you can imagine the effect of all this repetition on the half-clods. Too much information makes the half-clods reel, of course, and that often produces good results. If an issue is complex, many half-clods are sure to resent it. That is what helps our political agenda so much in the developed nations.

Salome-the-sister was the one who eventually stopped the pretensions of Antipater to the throne. She was a frustrated person, mainly because her brother would not allow her to marry one of his enemies, the Arab Syllaeus, and forced her to marry one of his courtiers, Alexas. The Herodian court was indeed a golden time for us, as the yellow-metal-loving half-clods would say. The intrigues that we were able to pull off there should be required study for all devils.

But I digress. [A stylistic flourish I did not expect. –ed.] So Salome, who hated Antipater, spied upon him. This caused a certain amount of discussion between devils. Some devils who are attached to famous half-clods begin to see them as clients and lose their damned perspective. We don't really care who wins if they all go to hell. I suppose the devils who worked with Antipater felt that he could have been more useful to us in the Palestinian Theater than that idiotic scrupe, Pontius Pilate, but that call is not ours to make, for which we can thank HSM. *Even to pretend to know better than the Infernal High Command should indeed be punished, as it was. But there were times when it seemed in these early days of the Invasion that troops were working at cross-purposes. That is a preposterous corollary of the Michaelist ideology and we must remember who is boss, after all. Hail Satan, etc.* [Emphasis added because it sounds like boilerplate Satanic interpolation. –ed.]

This busybody *yenta*-wannabe Salome invited Balthazar to come to meet her the morning after Antipater's rather inconclusive encounter with Caspar. She pretended she wanted to consult Balthazar, and had a few "experts" in tradition with her.

"I appreciate this chance to talk with you because I have always held that wisdom lies to the east of us." Salome would have made a great queen, as she was most ready to admit. Augustus' wife, Livia, was a personal friend of hers. Like some formidable women, she was very aware of her effect on others. I think she could have played the wonderful Medea in the Greek plays. She pronounced her words very slowly, as though they were all of great import.

"Your highness flatters a poor seeker of truth," said Balthazar. This is another example of Trinitarian hypocrisy. This Balthazar thought pretty well of himself, that can be demonstrated. His humble-pie act didn't fool even Salome, even if evidence suggests that the poor fool really believed it himself. [Typical devilish logic—we half-clods cannot win with them. Even the fact that Balthazar was sincere is used against him. -Informant]

"I would compare your visit to the story of another prophet from beyond the Euphrates, the famous Balaam." Salome said "Balaam" in a hushed tone and opened her eyes, very heavily mascaraed, I might add—the vanity of the strumpet! —very wide to indicate that she had somehow let the dragon out of the shell. [A difficult translation, really a kind of guess. -Informant]

"I am afraid that my brother Caspar probably knows who you are referring to, but I do not, ma'am. Your religion requires great study and I am just a beginner." Balthazar had no more idea of the story of Balaam and the asinine donkey than of the geography of hell, of course.

"Explain to him about Balaam," Salome said to one of the men standing by. She of course had no clue about the identity of Balaam, but was speaking according to a prearranged conversational script, like one of those plays half-clods make up in which all sorts of imaginary events are dealt with. [Or like presidents and prime ministers with talking points on teleprompters. –Informant] We angelic beings can only work with reality, not alternative models. [An interesting point about angelic intelligence. They do not know about fiction (except for lying) and the uses that thinking can make of fiction. –ed.]

"Balaam is the prophet from the country beyond the Euphrates who blesses Israel against the wishes of King Balak. You see, he was a worshipper of Adonai who could only say what Adonai wanted him to say even though Balak was paying him to curse the Chosen People." This was stated in a bland voice by an old codger who looked bored even as he said it. He was really happy, however, because he figured that he would be appropriately tipped for the bit part he was playing in the drama.

"A very interesting comparison," said Balthazar. "But do you believe that we have come here to bless the newborn king? We are here not to give but to receive. (Which was a lie, of course, because we all know about the three gifts.) [Another interpolation. –Informant] We are seekers of truth and not artisans of destiny. It is curiosity more than anything that has drawn us here. The stars lead us to conclude that there is something tremendous about this birth."

"But what about my stars? What do the stars say about my beloved brother? Surely you can tell us something." Salome had learned as a young girl to speak with pouted lips, but it really was pathetic at her age to see her begging the Magian to help her.

"Of course, we can. But first we must go to find out about this child. And then we shall have much to tell you, I think."

Balthazar could not have been as stupid as he was presenting himself. Nothing is worse than a sanctimonious half-clod who stands in our way. Even though he was resisting this awful woman, *she* thought he was being very kind to her because of his tone of voice and because of the ways their eyes met. Half-clod sympathy is a mystery to us because it involves all these stupid materialist tricks of trade. Two sets of gelatinous material [He means the eyes. –Informant] somehow communicate sympathy to each other, or anger or sullenness or boredom. It is all very hard to follow and typically complicated.

The interview was over. Salome should have poisoned this idiot Balthazar. Instead, she told her brother that Balthazar seemed to be forthright, even though Caspar had been seen intriguing with Antipater.

CHAPTER TWENTY-NINE:
HEROD AND MELCHIOR

Neither Caspar nor Balthazar really knew what was going on. They were excluded from the conversation Herod had with Melchior. This Melchior was a rogue who did not even let his colleagues in on a daring plan to trick the king. [Look who's talking. –Informant]

The true story was this way. Melchior had a private meeting with King Herod. Since he had that Oriental inscrutability about him, Herod was at first quite cautious.

"I have come to you in private, great king, because I would like to propose something neither my people nor yours should know about."

This sparked Herod's interest, of course, along with that of our agents.

"I think it unwise that the Jewish state at this time embark on a campaign of conquest. We have already seen the use the Greeks made of Alexander's meteoric career. Our countries need peace in order to progress. Great heroes shine in the firmament for their little while and then the rest of men have to work decades or even centuries to make up for the destruction they leave behind.

"In my opinion, the Child of Destiny that we have been

sent to visit by the whole Magian court will cause a great deal of problems in the world. He will change everything. In the interest of his kingdom, all other kingdoms will suffer. How can their history compare with a special vocation written in the stars? My colleagues are already enamored of the Child, saying that he will change the world. Order will be disrupted. It will be like the greatest earthquake our Terra has ever suffered."

Herod looked at him with pleasure bordering on infatuation. The fools we had on guard that night at first could not tell whether Melchior was lying. That came out at the court martial. A devil unable to detect the lack of veracity in a half-clod? *It was negligence, laziness, an obtuseness that represents the essence of the Michaelist heresy and its opposition to our Satanic Majesty's Eternal Rule.* [This last is italicized because it appears to be an editorial interpolation. –ed.]

"But, my friend, if this Child is really destined by fate or whatever to rule, how can we stop him?" Herod asked in one of his falsest tones.

"I have studied the stars all of my life, o king," replied Melchior. "I have seen how the configuration of stars and planets have all seemed to predestine an event, but a small circumstance manages to obstruct everything. If one knows that someone is destined to kingship, and prevents that person from living to maturity, one is able to upset even the plans of the stars. There is always that small window of opportunity in which bold spirits can act."

"But what must I do, Melchior?"

"You must permit us to act alone. I have seen that anyone who acts against this child will have a high price to pay for it if he is also a Jew. You, sire, are a Hellene and a man of the world, but your throne depends upon you also being a Jew. If you act against the child, there is a chance of a revolt. I have seen a configuration of planets and stars that represents a great threat to your kingdom, but I have also seen a possibility of great hope."

Here the meretricious Melchior was skating on the edge of truth. Yes, there was a great threat against the kingdom. Yes, there was great "hope." But the two were connected. The threat was the hope and the hope the threat. Presenting them as two different alternatives was really a lie. [Lessons on truthfulness from a demon! – Informant]

"As soon as we see the Child, we shall inform you of the best way to dispose of this threat, unless, of course, it is unnecessary to do so. However, I am relying on your honor, o king. You must not let my colleagues know that anything is out of the ordinary. Above all, do not let us be followed, neither by your men nor those of your son Antipater. You are aware, I presume, that your son has established contact with us separately."

The great king was not aware of this, but he was not about to let on about his ignorance. He merely nodded, and then said, "I assure you that I will allow you to act alone. But you must tell me why you are so concerned about our little kingdom."

"Your little kingdom, as you call it, is the center of civilization at this point. There is no place on earth more important right now. If we do not act carefully now, all may be lost."

The filthy liar was telling the truth, but it had a different meaning for his listener. The caution of the Magian was precisely the fear of the king. Herod was completely convinced by the foul trick of Melchior.

CHAPTER THIRTY: THE MAGI REACH THEIR GOAL

[Seems to be a different devil writing this—the conversational tone of the podcast is lost. –ed.]

Of course, the story has been manipulated by the Enemy to represent an anticipation of the Child's universal dominion. It is hard for me even to write about this chapter in the history of the Invasion, because all our resistance was useless. The meeting of the three Magi with Joseph, Miriam and the Child was not as bad as those cheap reproductions seen in the end of the year solstice greetings half-clods send around [Christmas cards – Informant; no kidding –ed.]

Of course, Antipater had sent spies to follow the Magi. This was an idea of one of our agents, somewhat at counter purpose of those who wanted to follow Herod's plan. You are no doubt all aware that sometimes despite ourselves and because of the Enemy, we work in contradiction to each other. You cannot be involved in human life without being immersed in contradiction. Some theorists have held that this is another benefit of Original Sin, but others say that it has a subtler cause: the mixture of spirit and flesh has lost its original harmony, whatever that might have been. There is a virus in hylomorphism, as one of the more abstract professors has put it. Flesh and Spirit were supposed to be in perfect harmony, a kind of refraction of the abominable Incarnation, where Spirit itself was joined to Matter. Because only the logic of humiliating love could justify something as undignified as communicating spirit to matter, it is beyond understanding for us. The absurdity of it! [A string of blasphemy deleted. –ed.]

The spies sent by Antipater ran into others sent by King Herod and were killed by them. There were five of those against ten of these. The men from Antipater were met by a party twice their number, using a formula that the old king had used all his life: double the evil and get a return. It was night on the road to Bethlehem, at a place where the road bends, an excellent terrain for an ambush. In the skirmish, all of the son's spies were killed but three of Herod's men were also dead—Antipater's Idumeans were fierce warriors—and four more were wounded.

One man was so frightened by the fighting, and so afraid at seeing men dying, that he ran away. We had a devil follow him the rest of his life, but he did not make it to Hell, sad to say. The other two men were so occupied with the wounded that they did not make it to Bethlehem until a few days later, and, most suspiciously and ironically, were entering into town when the Magi were already leaving. By the time they understood that the Magi had not gone back to Jerusalem and reported this to Herod, it was too late. The old king had them beheaded, of course. (Of the two, one made it to Hell because as he died he cursed the Triune Dictatorship {by another name, of course—he didn't know about Number Two and Number Three} and everybody in the world besides. The other, unfortunately, cried out a petition of mercy from the Enemy and was granted it—a painful lesson for all of us.)

Therefore, the Persian party made it to the encounter with Number Two "unaccompanied" by the Herodian conspiracy. Our own attempt to prevent the meeting was also unsuccessful. I have mentioned how our legions had to back away from Bethlehem because of adverse conditions. There were devils still there, of course, on the outskirts, but none of any rank. Therefore, HSM decided to send a special agent to follow the Magi.

Azazel was in charge of supervising and potentially sabotaging the Magi's visit to Bethlehem. He was an old hand in the Palestinian Theater. You will remember that he is mentioned in *Leviticus*, where he is identified either as an old goat or as a type of satyr. For this Azazel has received much mockery and it should be said that when we are working with half-clods we cannot expect "serene logic nor elegant abstraction." Human beings relate to other mammals. When they are angry with each other they call each other the names of other species. Some of them even prefer other species for their companions. It is mysterious for us who cannot even imagine half-clods as companions, let alone dumb brutes, but there is some kind of communication or sympathy of matter. Material things matter to them. [Unfortunate translation I think. - ed.] That explains how some half-clods will be inspired when their part of the earth is turned away from the sun and leaves the sky a certain color. [A sunset. -Informant; What can I say, X was not always so familiar with common sense or normality, I'm afraid.. -ed.]

The important thing about Azazel was that people believed that whenever they were alone in the desert, he could be present to them. In *Leviticus*, the expiatory animal sacrifice was somehow consigned to him. This has been variously interpreted to mean that it was given up for lost, but there was still a kind of charisma of evil associated with the name. That is why the old soldier was called in to supervise the troops in Bethlehem.

Things started well in the sense that murder was committed right away. One of the camel drivers of the Magi got into a drunken fight with one of the carriers, ostensibly because a girl had looked at both of them in an inn. Really it was because we wanted to upset the Magi. The altercation grew general and was noisy, until Balthazar intervened.

"You men are fighting about trifles and we are reaching the goal of a lifetime," he said, in a tone that half-clods take to convey great mystery. "Temptations are to be expected, because we will only see what we are going to see once in our lives. There is dark, secret opposition to what we are doing here; cosmic forces that are beyond our comprehension hate the blessing we will receive. We must choose now blessing or curse. I will say no more."

Of course, this made the men afraid, especially since most of them were not sure about what "cosmic" meant. They apparently thought Balthazar had mysterious, magical powers and were probably afraid he would make their clod limbs wither or whatever. As a result of this check, Azazel concentrated on the animals awhile. His account is terribly boring, because he must have been in the desert too much, observing the wildlife while good devils were observing wild living. But I will give you a snatch of his writing here.

"The rebellious nature of the camels helped us in the last leg of the journey. I made the camels hear the hissing of a million serpents. Their fear communicated one to another to the point that they became unmanageable. Then I made them see wolves stalking the caravan. Every shadow frightened them. Three camels bit carriers, which caused a great deal of ruckus. Then we made some cold breezes, and the animals were frightened when they saw the vapor that accompanied their breathing. They made strange cries, as if they were desperate. They knocked their drivers with their heads as if pleading with them not to go on. The drivers had no compassion, however, and drove the beasts mercilessly." [You'd know the only compassion in the whole devilish business is shown to animals. –ed.]

I will have you note this business of "strange cries, as if they were desperate." If that does not sound like some half-clod who has been looking too much at the moon, I don't really care to know. Azazel became a caricature of himself. Camels, camels, camels. Meanwhile they got to Bethlehem and then the Enemy cheated again. They were "led by the star to the place where the child was." The star was one of our erstwhile comrades, an angel named Uriel. [Suddenly an explanation of the star as an angel, but no further details. – ed] And Azazel was counting it a victory that a bag of dates fell off a stressed animal. Or that another rolled in the sand with the bread the men had bought in the Jerusalem market.

So, Uriel brought them to a small house Joseph had built on Nathan's property, a few steps distant from the miserable cave where Spirit had descended into the mire of flesh. [I delete here a devilish gibberish that makes this space the moral equivalent of "expletive deleted." – Informant]

There was an air of ritual to the meeting. First the three Magi descended, or rather their animals knelt down and the men stood up off the saddles. The precision showed by the Magians was probably due to the ceremonial aspect of their profession. The coordination of the camels was a cheap trick by the Enemy, making it seem that the beasts themselves were in awe of the child, and were genuflecting to some awesome power because of a sort of animal intuition into the mysteries of this miserable material world. The camel drivers and the porters were of course duly impressed, which seems to have been enough for *You Know Who*.

The first of the Magi to approach the child was Caspar. From a bag on the saddle of the camel he extracted a gold ingot marked with the curlicues of Persian writing on it. The inscription said, "To the king of kings." I am happy to note that Joseph later sold the piece in Alexandria for less than what it was worth and that each successive owner succumbed to a feverish and fatal pursuit of greater wealth. Six out of ten were damned. The powerful black man kneeling in the dirt before the poor woman and the squirmy piece of flesh that incarnated one third of the Triune Tyranny was not without irony, but it was painful to behold. Azazel was so stultified by the gesture and its meaning that he could only gape at it impotently.

Half-clods are symbolizing creatures. We all know that, but sometimes it is hard for us to appreciate how their fellow-feeling with matter allows them to read into things. In this case, of course, theologians have weighed in with their usual repetitiveness. The gold was a symbol of tribute to a king. The Magi were acknowledging the Pretender as the King of Kings. Unfortunately, it was not that simple.

Remember that this Magus was not born one. He was a slave, one who never let go of his feelings about being sold as chattel. His gold bar was the same value as the price that had been paid for him. Balthazar had paid dearly for young Casper. And the Nubian never forgot it. Giving the equivalent of the price of his slavery to the Pretender was symbolic beyond the idea of tribute. It was the price of his soul. It was, to our point of view, tragic and disgusting, but it is well we bear in mind that the half-clods can sometimes summon up a good deal of poetry in gesture. The gold was a spiritual tribute and, we can say regrettably, quite definitive. The man had given his life over to the Pretender. He didn't even need continuing contact to breathe a kind of communion with the purposes of the Invasion. We must learn from such events.

Next came Balthazar, who also had a saddle bag with a precious content, as it turned out. If only Azazel had let off on the animal kingdom nonsense, he might have inspired one of the camel riders to steal these gifts. It would have made a great show, the Magi digging in the bags to take out a handful of sand. Balthazar approached the mother and child on his knees, rather a disgusting display, and then set before them an ornate silver box encrusted with pearls that contained pellets of an incense from far off India.

Half-clods are obsessed with that aspect of materiality that is olfactory. This is something so far removed from Spirit that it escapes our attempts to understand it. What could be so interesting in how a hardened piece of this material world can be burned causing fragments to clutter the space around the clods and that these are perceived by the nose of these creatures sometimes as a most agreeable odor. Why would a certain aroma be associated with worship? The effrontery of the half-clods in assigning an odor to us is a special insult inspired by our Enemy. As if we would smell of sulfur! Just because it is an unpleasant odor, the half-clods try to connect it with us, who are pure spirits? They are the ones who have odor, we do not. [Many thanks for that clarification, Señor Diablo. –Informant]

The theologians have always emphasized that the incense was symbolic of adoration. Frankincense was used as an offering to the divine. The Magian spiritual universe was quite complicated compared to the Covenant of the Chosen People, but traces of true religious spirit were buried within the mythological rubble. Amid the garbage, a lot of which was the painstaking work of our agents, there was an idea of communion with the Tyranny, not by that name, but in essence the Deity.

Balthazar had pursued the Deity all his life. He had the pretension that he was one of the Chosen Ones, a select mystic company that walked in another kind of dimension through the sordid streets of the world. They are disgusting, of course, presuming a mystic communion with Spirit that they have no right to, the half-clods!

The incense came to an interesting use. As soon as Joseph, Miriam and the Pretender got to Egypt, Joseph sold the incense box for a pittance. The incense Miriam wrapped up in scraps of cloth and tucked in folds of Joseph's garments. This was a small gesture, but it resulted in the man carrying about himself an atmosphere of prayer. It was a wretched little trick, and the only touch of royal bearing to a life of hard work knocking pieces of wood together. The man's very sweat—remember all material life flows with water—mingled with the smell of incense.

Lastly came Melchior, who walked on his spindly old man's legs. A strange man, walking with a slow pace that seems like he is trying to imitate the eternal wheels of what the half-clods call Providence. The baby looks up at the old man. It is the meeting of generations, an encounter of *Weltanschauung* (considering that the Incarnation was greeting a person descended from Buddhists) —call it whatever cutesy thing you want. [And why not German? –Informant] The old man is weeping; tears are running down his cheeks like a little waterfall. Too—too—shy making, of course. *Schmerz* and *schmaltz*. The Enemy never gives up on this stuff. It's the viscera—the half-clods recognize some truths only in their guts.

So, this old man gets up to where the child is seated on the lap of his mother and then swoops down, as if falling, and kneeling extends a wrinkled gray hand, the skin like papyrus, to the foot of the Pretender and then lifts it gently to his lips. This kiss has somehow entered the junk locker of half-clod imagination called the collective unconscious and shows up periodically in works of art. It is an image of the destruction of human dignity wedded to this world.

Melchior had reason to be proud of the knowledge he had from so many different traditions. But his abject obsequiousness before the Pretender obliterated any hubris he might have mustered within his decrepit old body, wasting away even as he walked so reverently to his meeting. We lost him there. If there is no hubris, there is hardly a chance for us with the older half-clods. Lust is reliable up to a point, so is Avarice, but there is nothing like Pride.

Appropriately, the old man gave an alabaster vase of myrrh. He was so close to death, of course he gives something related to death. The Child would die, is what he was saying. Instead of being repulsed by the idea of Spirit attached to putrid flesh, the old man rejoiced in it.

"For our salvation, Thou hast wedded thyself to this clay," said the old man in a whisper. The baby stared at him. "Blessed be the Almighty and His inscrutable plans!"

One would like to know what the mother thought of these words as she took the small alabaster vase. It, too, was sold in Egypt so that the three of them, the Pretender and his "court," could eat. The Egyptian who bought the myrrh was impressed with it, at least. He knew his myrrh, and could tell it was from the coasts of the Indian Ocean. The old merchant kept the alabaster vase for his own funeral, which was after the death of the Pretender. Crazy by then, the rich old man claimed that he had seen the myrrh glow through the alabaster for a day and two nights in the spring of the nineteenth year of the reign of Tiberius. We all know what happened then.

CHAPTER THIRTY-ONE: THE SLAUGHTER OF THE INNOCENTS

Meanwhile, Herod's court was a hotbed of activity. The king was still waiting for the Magus Melchior. Something about that aged Persian had inspired confidence in the old fool Herod. He was waiting for the three stooges to come back and tell the tyrant where the Little Threat to his Throne was being rocked to His sleep. This note is jarring for us, but the Pretender needed sleep. It was not as if he would only feign sleep, like we do when we take the appearance of a man. He needed all that human nature needs. An intolerable idea, spirit chained by matter and in such ridiculous ways: hunger for food, need for sleep, thirst. That is the bizarre kind of Enemy we fight—one which stoops so low as to be *beneath* angelic nature.

The Magi slept also, but not well. All three of the men had nightmares the night of the day they saw Number Two. Casper woke up in the middle of the night and thought he heard the howling of jackals which increased in volume to the point he swore they were just outside the luxurious tents that the three "kings" had put up in Nathan's yard. Balthazar had a dream of a dust storm that trapped them in their tents as their drivers and camels left the Magi behind. Melchior had a dream of a dragon seated outside the entrance to his tent. All three eventually, and with exaggerated caution, stepped out into the night.

"We must go, brothers," said Casper.

"I feel evil approach," said Melchior.

"Tell the men to pack," said Balthazar.

"But we cannot go back to Herod," said Casper.

"We must take a different route," said Melchior.

"Why do you say that as if I would resist?" said Balthazar. "We must quit here as soon as possible."

The devils watching them made the camel drivers and slaves of the three Magi very hard to awaken. Then they tried to inspire the servants to stubborn refusal. But there was a contagion of fear in the air, no doubt the work of the Enemy. Before dawn the Magi were ready to go.

In Jerusalem, Herod, who was waiting for his spies, had a very bad night. There should have been a messenger from Bethlehem. He decided that something or someone had foiled his plans. Likewise, Antipater was nervous as a cat and his father could tell from his son's eyes that he was guilty about something. Son was thinking that the father had killed his men and father was thinking the opposite. Both were more right than wrong, of course, but the tension was too much for them.

As soon as we had been aware that the three were slipping away, we had agitated in the court for something to be done. [Obviously a new writer because of the narrative "we." –ed.] Antipater had a nightmare that evening of the Magi in disguise riding black horses like thieves back to Persia. He interpreted this to mean that Persia was going to invade Palestine. We use these half-clods but we have to learn not to allow any detail to be completely in their hands. With this dream, Antipater woke up and plotted until morning thinking of how to use the Romans as a shield against the Persians and then betray them to the Persians who might set him up as a satrap. (Duh! as the clodlings would say.)

Scouts were sent to Bethlehem to make reconnaissance. Herod, a treacherous man, naturally suspected treachery. He still thought Melchior his man, but thought Casper and Balthasar had caught on to their colleague's opposition to the child. Nobody could be more intriguing than the king and so he wove a conspiracy theory out of thin air. Again, he was certainly correct in the big picture, but the details were absurd. For instance, he imagined Melchior gagged and bundled up on the back of a camel. He shared this hallucination with his son Antipater, who suggested scouts be sent out to see what was happening in Bethlehem. He figured his own men had enough of a lead to get there first.

It was too late. Several soldiers got near Bethlehem and we hoped they would pursue the Magi, who had gone west to the coast and then to Egypt. From Egypt the scum sailed to Cyprus and then to Antioch, safely out of Herod's reach. They sold their camels in Alexandria and freed all but a few of their servants and took a very long route home.

Two days later, scouts from Ashkelon raced in to tell the King that a caravan of Magi had passed at incredible speed during the night. This news had to wait to be told until King Herod had had his breakfast. He had been up drinking the night before. Perhaps he had had a premonition the Magi would betray him. That would explain why he got so drunk with Dionysius, his Greek philosopher, and a few favorites. After such debauchery, the old creep would have a queasy stomach and a headache. Another of the benefits of mixing spirit with matter: matter can revenge itself on spirit. His pains in the loins had already started, which had a symbolic congruence. One of the constant sources of pain and suffering in his life originated in the same place.

The King was in bed until noon. His bodyguards turned away all sorts of messengers sent to the royal boudoir. I am speaking about those awful Galatian guards that Herod had inherited from Cleopatra, Queen of Egypt. They were monsters, of course, and headstrong and proud as only Celts can be. [Shocking comment. –ed.] When they were not killing someone for Herod, they were trying to kill each other. We trained them well.

Ennakenda was the chieftain in charge of the guards. As a child he had seen the denouement of the Cleopatra saga, which ended so tragically for us. He remembered witnessing as a child outside the royal quarters and the rush of the guardsmen to and fro when Octavius sent the guard to see whether his suspicions of the intended suicide of his captive queen were correct.

Of course, there has been doubt lately in sophisticated circles that the story of the asp is true. For us, the real story of the queen's shocking repentance as she was dying on the gold bed dressed up as a Pharaoh is too doleful to repeat here. What is interesting is that Ennakenda's father, Kenda-enna, was one of the first to see the dead Cleopatra. He reported that he had not seen any tooth marks on the body, which he had studied with some care. That night Kenda-enna got very drunk and started a fight with another Galatian, who killed him.

Thus, Ennakenda's memories of his father were

intermixed forever with the death of Cleopatra. He was a child, and not a very bright one. Not so very bright children nearly always become not so very bright men. Only Ennakenda was not just stupid, he was aggressively ambitious, and a liar of international standing. Under our care he had made sure that no savagery would be too outré for him or stand between him and his desire to be the chieftain of his clan.

He had grown old in vice and was cruel in a manner that would have shamed the so-called beasts without reason. His heart was more enraged than a lion's, his hands bloodier than a butcher's, his eyes more venomous than any asp, his tongue more flexible in lies than an eel in a river, his mind more malevolent than the scorpion's, to use what the half-clods call poetic imagery. [I think you've got the idea by now, the devil-narrator is showing off his knowledge of the animal kingdom. What do you expect from a textbook? –Informant]

Ennakenda was called to the presence of King Herod when the latter finally was convinced that the three stooges had vamoosed. [An awkward rendering, but the original is quite colloquial. –Informant] Poor Herod could never remember Ennakenda's name. He sent for him saying, "Where is that big Celt, the Galatian? You know who I mean." Then when the old warrior's name was announced in the presence of the king, he could hear Herod bellow, "I didn't send for a serving girl," for the name didn't sound masculine to the royal personage. Then the matter was cleared up, as it always was, and Ennakenda came into the presence of the king.

The idiot always wanted to say something about Cleopatra. He always started to say it, but the king would cut him off. So it happened this time.

"I am reminded by this emergency of an incident that I recall from my childhood," Ennakenda began quite pompously.

"Never mind that!" shouted Herod, who could barely understand Ennakenda's heavily accented Greek, and had never, unlike Cleopatra, learned the dialect of his guards.

Ennakenda was hard of hearing, and did not catch Herod's growling.

"I was such a little boy. What did I know about the Queen of queens, the extraordinary Cleopatra, the most beautiful woman in the world?"

"Damn you, Ennakendus, we must take action. There is a child in Bethlehem who must be killed!"

"I beg your pardon, sire, but I remind you that my name is Ennakenda, not Ennakendus."

"Must you continue to try my patience!" screamed the king.

"My intention is only to correct a misconception regarding my name," said the old bucko with a brogue beyond the powers of exaggeration, which is actually a much-favored thing among certain clodlings.

"Your misconception has to do with thinking that where your head is connected to your big body is a permanent thing," said the king.

Somehow this got through. Ennakenda rushed to the quarters of the guards and gave a speech that lasted two hours. The kingdom was in trouble, evil walked the streets, and gloom was bearing down on the king and therefore his much-hated personal guard. He assumed that all could gather the message he meant to convey and he did not need to be more explicit, etc. At the end, he mentioned that the guard must raid the village of Beth-something and they must pretend to be the Sicarios, or Zealots or whatever you wanted to call them, and kill every child under the age of well he wasn't exactly sure about that and they should probably use their own judgment, if they knew what he meant, and he hoped that included the majority, etc. A more bumptious, pretentious and stupid speech could not have been invented by a devil. [Now that is saying something. -Informant]

After the speech there was the question and answer period, which for the Galatians was *de rigueur*—remember they are a Celtic people. Did the Taoiseach—or whatever they called him—know for certain the name of the town? Of course he didn't. Did he have some sense of the age range of the monstrous child who might be a threat to the throne of Good King Herod? This question sparked laughter among the disgraceful Celts. Meanwhile the devils stood around, and instead of making the session end shortly, seemed to enjoy Ennakenda's discomfiture. Idiots, Michaelist traitors, unworthy possessors of the angelic nature, etc. They are all consigned to a very special place in the kingdom.

Meanwhile, of course, the Enemy had sent a messenger to Joseph in a dream. The man, always responsive to impulses of that type, had immediately prepared the donkey and the few possessions the miserable family had for a flight. Precious time was wasted, while the Galatians began to argue with each other, which they liked to do very much. In fact, Ennakenda had to restrain one of his more enthusiastic supporters from burying a hatchet in the skull of a man who seemed to ask too many questions.

The Galatians were not underway for several hours. Of

course, part of that time was spent verifying that the town was Bethlehem and not Bethsaida or Bethany—Ennakenda had not been certain and had said all three names during his discourse to the troops, thinking that whichever had the most resonance among the soldiers was probably the one. A devil made one of the officers go back to the king and ask, with a peculiar consequence. "The royal personage of course took umbrage." That was Ennakenda's explanation of why the messenger he sent to the king came back with only one earlobe in place and the other in his fist. He had been told to present himself to his commander and ask if that was a look he thought would "work" for him, too.

Even you all know that the Galatians were late, that Joseph and Mary had fled with the Pretender. Nothing would do but to spill as much blood as possible. The crazed guards massacred children in a rampage but it gave little solace to HSM. The bird had flown, the prisoner had escaped, the hand had to be folded, the game was over, and we had lost the first skirmish of the war of wars. [Skirmish! There you have the devil putting a spin on the wreckage of their best attempt to block the birth of the Son. -Informant] The last gambit to occur to the High Command involved the attempt we shall look at in the next chapter.

CHAPTER THIRTY-TWO:
THE END OF THE BEGINNING

When it was obvious that Ennakenda's men were wasting time in Bethlehem, we alerted Herod that the Galatians were engaged in useless slaughter—although it is hard to believe that any slaughter can be useless to us. [Doesn't mention the children went to heaven. –ed.] It was, alas, too late. There are all sorts of stories about how the trio of Joseph, Miriam and the *enfant terrible* were chased through the crossing to Egypt by the powers of darkness, but they are exaggerations.

Obviously, the bandits whom some devils moved to try to ambush the pilgrims were hardly what the writers of legends pretend. They were incompetent half-clods, whose envy of each other was counterproductive. The rag-tag bunch of fools who ended up skirmishing with a Roman Legion on the march is hardly worth our time and reflection. These are issues of other, more specialized investigations, however. The whole story of the oasis and the trio turning invisible, for instance, just shows how unfairly the Opposition was playing the game. Remember that the invisibility had to do with Faucus' whirling himself into a sandstorm when the child cried because he sensed his mother's fear. The *pain* of the Divine Pretender so frightened Faucus that he spun into a tornado of fine sand that made all visibility impossible. That is different than invisibility as such, but don't expect such distinctions from half-clod legends. All in all the Enemy played many unfair tricks on us and our useful fools in the story of the famous Flight into Egypt. And this is not to speak of the Angelic Legion that accompanied the family to Alexandria, more angels than had been present in the Exodus!

In that city, some attempts to frustrate the eventual return of the Pretender to his Promised Land simply did not work. There was a plan to inspire Joseph to take Miriam to Rome. Lost in the dark heart of the Roman imperium, where our forces were so much in control, the couple and their child would not be able to do anything in Palestine. Now, of course, some strategists have argued post-facto that the "immigration gambit," as it was called, was not workable because it pushed the problem away and did not resolve it. As soon as Joseph arrived in Alexandria, cohorts of enemy custodians (especially Cherubim and Thrones) were seen to surround the person of Number Two and made it next to impossible to insinuate anything into the mind of that narrow-minded monk, his protector, the famous carpenter. (It was also unfortunate that the devil in charge apparently thought that avarice was the way into Joseph's heart, promising him heaps of gold in Rome, etc., which was a dubious strategy.)

These materials are about the first phase of the resistance to the Invasion and it is perhaps pedantic and self-serving to defend a particular line of attack with which this author was involved in formulating. Nevertheless, I feel compelled to say that the "Roman" strategy was not an altogether illogical one. In a strange land, a man can forget his religion, his customs, and his values. He can fall into vices, like drinking or loose women. His alienation is a tool that we can use to destroy his soul. Perhaps not enough was invested in this gambit. If we could have detached Joseph from his "world" we would be able to change the *Weltanschauung* and mission of his purported offspring.

But of course the Jewish settlement in Egypt had too much critical mass for us to pull off the separation of Joseph and company from his heritage. There was also the erroneous and possibly Michaelist hypothesis, known for its author, the hapless Asmodeus, which held that Number Two would wait until manhood, like the infamous Moses, before initiating military action against us. It turned out that "out of Egypt I have called my son," really only meant a brief stay in the country.

And so, the end of the first phase of the Invasion. It is considered a tactical victory to have sent the Child into exile at the beginning. HSM took his revenge on the House of Herod and Act One came to an end with a suitable bloodbath. When the old king died, he took Ennakenda with him, much to the chagrin of the Galatian. HSM saw fit to chain the two together forever, evil genius and evil idiot never to be parted.

EPILOGUE

[Here the file ends quite abruptly. A denouement that leaves one dissatisfied, if you ask me. Perhaps that is why at this point the archive includes an audio of a satanic laugh track digitally reproduced, the noise of which I will never forget. –Informant]

The files are obviously incomplete. There is no document that deals with the Presentation of Our Lord in the Temple, when Simeon and the old prophetess recognize the child. Maybe some of the files were impossible to locate or translate. Perhaps someday they may turn up. But that will not be on my watch, I believe.

After I had prepared this manuscript with my own remarks interspersed with the commentary of the man I helped to escape hell—for that is how serious I believe this to be—I was contacted by a mysterious woman.

One morning I went over to Mass at the church. Mary Hogan introduced her busy self into the sacristy while I was preparing myself for the sacred rites. I turned to her a bit sternly, because I don't like distractions while I say my prayers and vest before I offer the sacrifice.

"Yes, Mary?"

"There was someone here to see you."

"And?"

"I told him or her, I couldn't tell by the voice and you know how my eyesight is suffering, that you would be over in a few minutes, that it was your custom to come over almost exactly at the hour of the service."

"And?"

"The person could not wait, but left this note. I can't make head or tails of it," she said, as she handed me the envelope.

It was a note scrawled in very poor letter, I must say, but nevertheless placed inside an unsealed envelope. I didn't ask Mary why she presumed to look at the note because I did not want to go out on the altar in a hostile mood. Without opening the envelope myself, I shoved it in my pocket. She was upset, as I knew she would be, that I didn't look at it.

"Thank you, Mary," I said.

This also was not sufficient, apparently. She made a face and moseyed out of the sacristy while I resumed vesting.

I waited until after breakfast to open the envelope. It was a surprise to me. I figured it was some Yank trying to do some genealogy. They'll show up here and expect a full list of their ancestors and any cousins in the immediate neighbor while they wait for it. Apparently, they are unaware that priests must eat sometimes to keep body and soul together. And they have such a time about the spelling of names and who was related to whom. If they would pour over the litany of saints like they do the names in their family tree, we would all be better off.

But the note was not about genealogy. It was anonymous, which made me almost throw it away, because parish life has taught me to ignore anonymous letters. Nevertheless, I read what it said several times.

> Dear Father,
>
> I know that he went to you before he passed on. And that he gave you some of his "investigations." You cannot know my name and I will only say that I work for a big Internet company. We worked together, ------- and I. His cubicle was next to mine and sometimes both of us would be there in the office after hours, although the company we work for is not strict about things like schedules.
>
> He never told me what he was up to, but I could tell it was dangerous. The bosses also were somehow alarmed even though he was one of the few geniuses on staff in this country. There were visits and some people who came to see him were quite disturbing (besides looking disturbed themselves). Several times it seemed like he was on the brink of telling me a secret and then was stopped short. I was, I guess, a little sweet on him. And I think he regarded me as at least a trusted acquaintance.
>
> Of course, his health steadily weakened. I did know he was in touch with you, although he hesitated to tell me because he said there were enemies within and without the company. I found a key on my desk the first day he did not show up for work, not that I was in the habit of such prying, but something told me to look for a clue about his absence. For some time, I had no idea what it was for and was about to ask around

when I thought better of it.

Later I discovered that it was to a desk in an abandoned cubicle that I saw him use on odd nights. He would hop from one computer to another some nights, carefully limiting his work time to throw any surveillance off the scent. They discovered later that the cameras in our workplace had been moved slightly so that there were some corners out of the way of the Big Brother vigilance this company thrives on. I am sure that he did that. He was an extremely clever man, although quite tortured. Of course, I presume you know that he drank a great deal, too.

In the desk I found some thumbnail drives that I am gradually opening up. Some of it was stuff that sounded like Kafka on meth. Creative writing, or so I thought at first. All from the devil's point of view, reports from the demons in Nazareth, etc. There was a whole slew of documents, if I can call them that, about the "Temple rendezvous." After reading them over a number of times, I realized they were speaking of the Finding in the Temple. (I went to Catholic grade school in the States.)

I know that I am being watched. My hope is that I will be able to copy some of the material and get it to you. I feel it should be seen and then perhaps destroyed. But I have discovered that I am being monitored. There were cameras in my house, in my work cubicle, in my car and even connected to my microwave. Somebody doesn't want me to look through what ------- left in that desk. After I cleared it out it was suddenly moved out of the office one day into what is called the laboratory. They are looking for something.

Pray for me, Father. I'm afraid ------ died before his time and I might join him soon. He took care of me, so that I can be on my own now. I will try to be in contact with you.

Since I received this missive, I have not seen hide nor hair of anyone who might be the person involved. I have no further files to print. My thinking is that the rest of the archives dealt with the rest of the story of Our Savior, but I really cannot say.

I would publish the leaks, of course, but I do not have them. So the G----- people, as I call them, including the one whom I mentioned in my preface, who keep calling and asking about my friend have no real reason to bother me more. I wonder sometimes if "they" got the girl. I pray that she somehow got some of the dragon's treasure that X. had in Bitcoins or whatever they are called and escaped. Of course, I do not mean that G----- had anything to do with the death of my friend or with his discoveries. But I try to warn his ex-colleagues away from their employment. The "deep and dark" net is a place of danger, I tell them.

I hope that the publication of these files does some good. Obviously, there were more we haven't seen. But what they tell us should strengthen our resolve to resist the powers of darkness and live like children of the light, as the good book says.

Finally, I ask for your prayers. I don't need to see any more files. My job is done. If anyone discovers the complement to this set of archives, I suggest he or she go to another priest, one not as old and tired as your servant.

May God bless us all and deliver us from evil, Amen. And may his soul and all the souls of the faithful departed rest in peace. Amen.

AC

The End

ABOUT ATMOSPHERE PRESS

Atmosphere Press is an independent, full-service publisher for excellent books in all genres and for all audiences. Learn more about what we do at atmospherepress.com.

We encourage you to check out some of Atmosphere's latest releases, which are available at Amazon.com and via order from your local bookstore:

The Embers of Tradition, a novel by Chukwudum Okeke

Saints and Martyrs: A Novel, by Aaron Roe

When I Am Ashes, a novel by Amber Rose

Melancholy Vision: A Revolution Series Novel, by L.C. Hamilton

The Recoleta Stories, by Bryon Esmond Butler

Voodoo Hideaway, a novel by Vance Cariaga

Hart Street and Main, a novel by Tabitha Sprunger

The Weed Lady, a novel by Shea R. Embry

A Book of Life, a novel by David Ellis

ABOUT THE AUTHOR

Richard Antall lives and works in Cleveland, Ohio, which is just as close to Hell as where you reside, but it has felt closer to him during the ten years he was writing this book. He has published three books of biblical reflections and a novel, *The Wedding* published in 2019 by the Lambing Press and read by dozens of his relatives. He thanks you for reading his book and will remember you in his prayers.

CPSIA information can be obtained
at www.ICGtesting.com
Printed in the USA
LVHW092204300721
694164LV00004B/155